THE GHOST

IN

APARTMENT

2R

THE GHOST IN APARTMENT 2R

A YEARLING BOOK

Text copyright © 2019 by Denis Markell
Cover art copyright © 2019 by Marco Guadalupi

All rights reserved. Published in the United States by Yearling, an imprint of Random House Children's Books, a division of Penguin Random House LLC, New York. Originally published in hardcover in the United States by Delacorte Press, an imprint of Random House Children's Books, a division of Penguin Random House LLC, New York, in 2019.

Yearling and the jumping horse design are registered trademarks of Penguin Random House LLC.

Visit us on the Web! rhcbooks.com

Educators and librarians, for a variety of teaching tools, visit us at RHTeachersLibrarians.com

The Library of Congress has cataloged the hardcover edition of this work as follows:
Names: Markell, Denis, author.
Title: The ghost in apartment 2R / Denis Markell.
Description: First edition. | New York : Delacorte Press, [2019] |
Summary: After discovering a ghost in his apartment, twelve-year-old Danny and his friends traverse Brooklyn's diverse neighborhood together to learn the spirit's origins and bring it to rest.
Identifiers: LCCN 2018042022 (print) | LCCN 2018048950 (ebook) |
ISBN 978-0-525-64572-6 (el) | ISBN 978-0-525-64571-9 (hc) |
ISBN 978-0-525-64573-3 (glb)
Subjects: | CYAC: Ghosts—Fiction. | Apartment houses—Fiction. |
Family life—Brooklyn (New York, N.Y.)—Fiction. |
Brooklyn (New York, N.Y.)—Fiction.
Classification: LCC PZ7.M339453 (ebook) |
LCC PZ7.M339453 Gho 2019 (print) | DDC [Fic]—dc23

ISBN 978-0-525-64574-0 (pbk.)

Printed in the United States of America
10 9 8 7 6 5 4 3 2 1
First Yearling Edition 2020

To Charlie Sahadi, patriarch of the Sahadi family and inspiration for Sammy Haddad, who has welcomed generations of customers of all races, religions, and backgrounds to his store with the warmth and humor that is the best of Brooklyn

THE GHOST

IN

APARTMENT

2R

CHAPTER 1

THE GREAT INJUSTICE THAT IS HAPPENING TO ME

Okay, in the Grand Scheme of Things, as my favorite history teacher, Mr. Nordstrom, likes to say, maybe it's not a *great* injustice.

Or as my dad likes to remind me, "Do you know how many kids would kill to be in your situation?"

Because this is really just about a closet.

Which wouldn't be such a big deal, except it's where I sleep.

So, yes, there are kids much worse off than I am, and I totally get that. But for a normal thirteen-year-old kid living in Brooklyn, what happened to me is, I think anyone would agree, a pretty big miscarriage of justice. Not like being enslaved, or made to feel like a second-class citizen or anything . . . Well, that's not true. I *do* feel like a second-class citizen. At least in my family nest.

We live in what is referred to as a two-bedroom apartment, since there are two bedrooms.

Which seems like a stupid detail but is actually a major part of this story.

Because I have an older brother and a set of parents (one of each sex—I only mention this because my friend Kyle has two moms and I want to be fair), that means two bedrooms for four people.

Now, in a typical family, I would share the bedroom with Jake (that's my brother's name), but since we're six years apart, it was decided when I was a whining little kid that me being in there would be a distraction from Jake studying.

And then he was a teenager, and then it was *really important* that he have his own room because, well, "You'll understand when you're older."

Well, I am older now, and a brand-new teenager myself, and nobody is saying I need to have my own room.

Okay, I do have a room.

Kind of.

Once I was too old to stay in my parents' room, they took the closet near the front door and turned it into a room.

I mean, it's a nice closet, as closets go, with a sliding door and shelves and room for a small futon. So that's my room.

And please do not make any Harry Potter jokes, because I've heard them all. I remember when I was in like first grade and friends would come over and think it was neat, because they would have normal rooms and mine was so different. Or they had normal families and shared a room with a sibling. "You're so lucky!" they would say.

Yeah, lucky me. Sleeping in a closet.

You might think that this is the injustice I'm talking about, but honestly, I didn't mind it, because of a promise my father and mother made to me when I got big enough to start complaining about the situation.

The promise was that I would get Jake's room right after he went to college. Which seemed totally fair. And Jake was cool with it, too. It's our parents who made the decision that totally ruined my life and changed everything.

Because in my moral universe a promise is a promise. Not something you can take back because it's not convenient. My dad says that there's a difference between "never" and "not right now," but I think that's garbage.

Basically, what happened was that Jake got into Cornell University. Which is an amazing thing, and was his first-choice school, and he totally deserves to go. But Cornell, I found out, is unbelievably expensive. And we just don't have that kind of money. Jake got a scholarship (I guess all that studying paid off), so I thought everything was fine, until the day after we dropped him off at school. It was late August, and I still couldn't believe I was finally going to have a real room to myself. I was thinking about how weird it would be to not have Jake around, when my parents knocked on my closet door.

I hear my dad clearing his throat. Then: "We need to talk to you."

CHAPTER 2

LIFE IS NOT FAIR (LIKE I DON'T KNOW THAT)

I am willing to bet that in the life of any thirteen-year-old boy (and girl too, probably, but I wouldn't know because I am not a girl), there are few words as chilling as "We need to talk to you" when it's said by your parents.

Immediately you start going down the checklist in your head of all the things you might have done (or not done):

Okay, school hasn't started, so it's not about grades.

And I haven't shoplifted anything, or broken anything, or left the top of the peanut butter jar not screwed on so the next person who picks it up will drop it on the floor, making a mess (I ask you, who picks up a jar from the lid? Is that really my fault?).

But from the expression on their faces, it's not a "you did something wrong" situation, it's a "we've got bad news" one.

They usher me into the living room and sit me on the couch between them. This is bad. Somebody has died. Or they're getting a divorce. My armpits are pretty drenched by now, and I don't even know how bad it is.

"First of all," my dad says, "nobody's died."

"And we're not getting a divorce or anything," my mom adds. "It's nothing like that."

They hug me. Already with the hugging. Whatever it is, it is *not going to be good*.

"So what's the problem?" I ask.

My mom is a social worker, and she has this way of talking. Like just now, when she says, "Well, it's not really a problem if you look at it the right way. . . ."

At this point she stops talking and seems to take a great interest in a stain on the couch. "Um . . ." She doesn't even look at my dad when she says, "Martin, please."

"Okay," my dad begins. "You remember when your mom and Jake went on that tour of colleges?"

"Sure," I say. Mom and Jake took a bus through Massachusetts and Connecticut and upstate New York.

"Do you know how we were able to afford that trip?"

"Sure. It was going to cost too much money to stay in hotels, and then one of Jake's friends' moms told Mom about AirHotel. Where people rent out rooms and sometimes whole apartments to people visiting their city or town."

My mom jumps back in. "It was cool. And you know what? AirHotel is in Brooklyn too."

My mouth dries up. I can see where this conversation is going, and I really don't like it.

Dad quickly adds, "You know how expensive it's going to be to send Jake to Cornell."

"But he has a scholarship!" I protest.

"That's a huge help," Mom says. "But it doesn't take care of everything. Plus it gets really cold up there, so he's going to need a good parka."

My dad shoots her a look. "This isn't about the parka, Maureen. Please."

"I was just saying—"

"What are you *just* saying?" I ask, knowing perfectly well what they are just saying, but I want to force them to actually just say it.

"This is something we want to try. It might not work out, but it could help bring in some really needed extra money," my dad says.

Okay, nobody else wants to say it out loud. "What you're saying is you want to rent out Jake's room instead of giving it to me *like you promised.*"

I am very proud of myself that I got all that out without yelling.

My mom puts her arms around me, which only makes it

7

worse. My world is completely ruined. "We don't want to, sweetheart. We have to."

"Hopefully, it's temporary," my dad says. "I have that grant money coming, and then I can finish the film and—"

"That's going to take forever!" I moan.

My mother stiffens. "That's not nice, Danny."

My dad bites his lip. It was a low blow. He's been trying to finish his film for four years now. He didn't exactly see himself working as a freelance video editor when he finished film school all those years ago.

I turn to him. "I'm so sorry, Dad. I didn't mean it. It's just that a promise is a promise, and you promised me. I've waited years and years. Now I'll NEVER get my room!"

Okay, this time I can't get the whole sentence out without yelling.

I stomp off into my closet and try to slam the sliding door.

"You know, there are kids who have it a whole lot worse than you," my dad calls out.

"Not now, Marty," my mom says, and even though I can't see her, I'm sure she's rolling her eyes.

CHAPTER 3

WHAT'S SO SPECIAL ABOUT JAKE GOING TO THE BATHROOM?

I don't think it's just the room I was mad about. The thing is, this whole past year has kind of been all about:

Jake studying for his tests.

Jake going on trips with Mom, which started this whole mess.

Jake writing his college application essay, with "help" from Dad, who basically read a whole bunch of books like *How to Write the Perfect College Essay*.

Jake hogging the PlayStation. And Mom saying, "Honey, Jake is working very hard. He needs his time to relax."

"So why can't he play with me?" I'd ask again and again.

"Because he likes playing with his friends online," Mom said, as if she knew what she was talking about. All she was doing was repeating what Jake told her when she asked him why he wouldn't play with his little brother.

Then he takes the PlayStation with him to college.

I *thought* it was a Hanukkah present for both of us when we got it, but I guess I was wrong. And he got a new laptop from our grandparents because he'll "need it for college."

I got a gift card for our local bookstore. Yay.

I don't want to give the impression that Jake is a jerk, because he isn't. He's a great guy. And he's really nice to me, usually. I love my brother, but I was definitely super psyched for my Actual Not-a-Closet Bedroom moment.

So after we dropped Jake off at college I was ready to be the center of attention for once in my life—and now my parents pull this on me. Did they expect I'd just go, "Hey! That's great! No problem! I'll just live in my little closet and totally forget you *promised me* I'd get that room! And hey, no hard feelings about all the money going toward Jake's education, because clearly I'm not as smart and so what's the point of saving up to help me go to college?"

I should mention that in all honesty, I actually did say that to my folks. Perhaps with a tone that was slightly sarcastic. But I don't think it warranted them acting like I was some sort of ungrateful dirtbag.

"Just ask your brother," my dad said, laughing. "He was so mad when we had you. All we talked about was 'the baby.'"

I was ready for this. "I happen to have overheard you on

the phone with Uncle Arthur when you said how different it was with 'the second child,' Mom. *You* said you kept a journal every day for Jake, writing down everything he did, but by the time *I* came around you barely wrote anything."

Mom takes a deep breath. "It wasn't because we love him more . . . it was just that I was going for my master's when you were born and didn't have time. . . ."

"And what's your excuse, Dad?" I said. "You took like a hundred videos of Jake as a baby, eating, puking, going to the bathroom . . . and like four of me, usually with Jake holding me."

"I'm not going to get into an argument about us loving your brother more," my dad says evenly. "It's ridiculous. You just need time to adjust to the new reality."

There's nothing new about this reality. They just love my brother more.

CHAPTER 4

FINISH THIS SENTENCE: MY LIFE STINKS NOW BECAUSE . . .

So now instead of everything revolving around Jake, it's all about AirHotel and making the room perfect to attract guests. My mom spends every night looking at other listings in our neighborhood, seeing which ones are getting the most views and which months seem to have the most bookings. Of course, the holidays are very popular, and summertime. Since we don't have air-conditioning, there's a whole discussion about getting a small air conditioner, but it's decided that they'll hold off until the spring, when they should know if people are actually going to stay with us.

"How would you fill in this blank?" My mother is reading off a website set up to help AirHotel hosts make their spaces (as rooms or apartments are called) enticing. " 'Guests should stay at my place first and foremost because . . .'"

My dad looks up from the bar mitzvah video he's editing at his workstation. Okay, it's really just a laptop attached to a monitor and keyboard, but since he can't afford to rent office space, we call it his workstation. And he's editing some kid's bar mitzvah video because the parents are loaded, and they hired him to shoot it and make a fancy montage and everything.

No, this isn't my dad's dream job. When he graduated film school his advisor told him that he was going to be the next Steven Spielberg. I don't like to think about it too much because even though he says annoying things to me and gets all bent out of shape when I don't remember to clear the table or something, I know he just wasn't as lucky as some of his classmates. But he keeps at it, which is either really brave or really pathetic. I haven't figured that out yet.

It really is true that they need the money, so I play along.

"Could you repeat the question?" my dad asks.

"'Guests should stay at my place first and foremost because . . .'"

My dad takes off his glasses and rubs his eyes. "Hmm. How about . . . 'they will have a true Brooklyn experience in a warm family atmosphere'?"

My mother scrunches up her face. "It's good, but I was thinking 'it's quiet and ideally located.'" She types both in.

"Any other questions?" I ask.

"'My space is specifically suited to . . .'"

" 'People who think promises are things you don't have to keep'?" I suggest.

"Ha ha," my mom says. "I'm serious."

I get up and head to my closet. "So am I."

I pass my dad's screen. There's a scene with disco lights, a smoke machine, and people who look like they're in their twenties dancing with kids.

"Who are those guys?" I ask.

"Those are entertainers hired by the parents to dance with kids and make everyone feel like it's a party," my dad responds.

"That's their *job*?" I ask.

"Yep. And they earn a lot of money doing it."

Now the camera is panning across the room—there's an entire sushi bar set up, a hot dog stand, and a burger station. I let out a low whistle. "How much do you think the whole thing cost?"

My dad shakes his head. "Gotta be at least forty grand. The dad is an investment banker."

That's almost what it would have cost to send Jake to Cornell for a year without financial aid.

In case I didn't mention it, I go to public school. When my friends are bar mitzvahed, there's usually just a really nice party at their home.

My mother is not happy. "Could you guys please help here?" she grouses.

"I'm sorry," my dad says. "Tell me again."

"'My space is specifically suited to . . .'"

"'Couples and people visiting the city on college tours, or anyone who wants a true taste of Brooklyn'?" my dad offers.

My mom nods. "That's really good. See? You have good ideas too! That's a lot better than what I came up with."

I know my mom so well. This is her way of getting Dad to engage.

I guess that's what makes her a good wife. I wish she was as good a mom. Well, to me, at least.

That's probably totally unfair, and she'd be very hurt if she heard me say it. So I don't say it out loud, of course. But I do feel it.

Mom moves on. "Oh, dear. It says the room really needs to be uncluttered and simple-looking if we want good reviews. I think we have some shopping to do."

I see my dad's shoulders tense.

Mom has pulled up the Ikea website. That's where we get most of our furniture. And looking at the photos on the AirHotel website, we're not alone.

She walks into Jake's old room and starts making a list.

"Remember, we're on a budget . . . ," my father calls from his workstation.

Next stop: Ikea, the Magic Kingdom of Brooklyn Bedrooms!

CHAPTER 5

ONE BIG MELTING POT WITH SWEDISH MEATBALLS

When most families go to Ikea, they pile into the car and head over.

For us, it's not so easy. We don't own a car, so we borrow my grandparents' from out in the suburbs.

It's not too far to drive to Ikea. We find a space in the garage and head upstairs. I love Ikea. The little fake rooms, with all those perfect accessories and cool prints on the walls. I would love to live there.

But today is different, since we're here to decorate the room that was supposed to be mine. I guess all Jake's worldly possessions are going to go somewhere else. We're even getting a new bed, because his is kind of beat up.

I can't help myself.

"So if we have the money to buy all this stuff," I say, "why do we need to rent out the room?"

My mother bends down. "Danny," she says.

I guess I should mention that my folks are kind of tall, and Jake is too. I still haven't hit my growth spurt, or so the doctor said at my last checkup. Maybe I'll always be short.

Anyhow, my mom is a lot taller than I am, so she has to bend over to look straight into my eyes. "This is going on our credit card. We're just hoping that the people who stay will pay enough."

I pick up a drinking glass that looks expensive but costs only $1.99. "So you're gambling."

My dad is putting six of the $1.99 glasses in our cart. "No, it's an *investment*."

We load up on everything the AirHotel site says will help us get good reviews from our "guests," even stuff that *isn't* for the bedroom: a fabric shower curtain with a liner, a cute area rug, a toilet seat (A new toilet seat? Really?), a framed print of something abstract and Swedish, and new silverware.

"We can get the hair dryer at the drugstore," Mom says.

"What the heck do we need a hair dryer for?"

"I was reading on the site about a guy who had four girls staying at his house and he didn't have one. These are the little things people care about."

I kind of stopped listening after the "four girls staying at his house" part. I cannot imagine a weirder situation than sharing our apartment with four girls.

"So you're saying that we could have four girls—" I begin.

"Don't be ridiculous," my dad says.

Whew.

"Maybe two, three at the most, if one sleeps on the couch in the living room," he adds.

I am hating this more and more.

We get all the numbers for the bed and the new night-stand. We're even getting a new desk. These are large things that have to be picked up downstairs. Before we leave, we go to the restaurant and have lunch.

This is always my favorite part of visiting the Brooklyn Ikea. It's like a little picture of Brooklyn, with all these people from different cultures eating together. You'll see a Jamaican family with a baby, and next to them a Chinese family with four older girls and a little boy. And over there, an Indian family buying stuff for their daughter to go to college (yes, I'm nosy and look in people's carts). There's a pair of newlyweds, the cliché Midwestern couple. You can hear like a dozen different languages, but everyone is saying the same thing. Cranky babies are the same in any language. Tired parents snapping at each other don't need a translation. When the newlyweds start bickering about which end table to buy, I see the parents in each group exchange knowing smiles.

I order the same thing every time: Swedish meatballs with

mashed potatoes. I see it on trays around the room, all of us from practically every country on the globe, eating Swedish meatballs.

That's Brooklyn for you. I mean, there are plenty of neighborhoods in Brooklyn where you'll see only one ethnic group or another, but when we get together in one place, somehow we all get along.

Well, everyone except my mom. She orders a salad, because she thinks it's healthier and feels the need to say this out loud every time. I guess that's *another* Brooklyn for you (the annoying one).

It's a little weird to be here without Jake, and not to be talking about him and college and everything. But Mom is too busy making sure she's got everything on her checklist and Dad is worrying about the traffic going back.

We get everything we need into the car and head home. The bed alone is really heavy (even though it's in pieces), so Dad has arranged for our super to help bring it upstairs to our apartment. When I say "our super" it sounds like he's our personal superhero. In a way he is. But he's really just the superintendent of the building. Which means when anything goes wrong in the apartment, he's the one to call.

Gabriel is a really cool guy. Even though my dad didn't ask, he's brought his tools. He knows my dad isn't the greatest at building things.

Like I said, our personal superhero.

Mom and I start unpacking the new stuff for the kitchen. She looks at her list. She loves lists. I don't think anything gives her as much joy as crossing stuff off a list. I think she makes lists sometimes just to be able to cross stuff off.

"We need to make an appointment with the photographer," she says to herself.

"Why can't we just take the pictures ourselves?" I ask.

"Well, we could. Some people do. But these people do it for a living. They know how to make rooms look bigger. They have all these tricks to make it look as nice as possible."

"Sounds expensive," I say.

"Actually, AirHotel provides it for free," my mom says.

"Great. Some guy is going to come over and make the place look perfect for groups of girls to come stay with us."

"I wish you wouldn't fixate on that girl thing. I never should have mentioned it." My mom is sounding irritated. Not at herself. At me.

I walk by the room that should have been mine and see that Gabriel and my dad are assembling the bed frame.

All of a sudden, as I stand in the door, a chill comes over me. Like there's a drop in the temperature. Like someone just turned on an air conditioner. But like I mentioned, we haven't gotten one yet. And it's early September.

I rub my arms. "Do you feel that?"

My dad doesn't look up from holding the frame in place so Gabriel can tighten the nuts holding it together. "Feel what?"

"It got cold all of a sudden," I say.

Gabriel is drenched in sweat. He rubs his T-shirt sleeve against his forehead and laughs. "Not here, man. If you got some cold air I wish you'd share it with me."

My mom calls from the kitchen. "Are you okay? Do you think you're coming down with something? I can take your temperature."

I step out of the doorway and I'm hot again. "No, I'm okay. Guess I just imagined it."

But I didn't. It was like the doorway was a different temperature from the rest of the room. Weird.

CHAPTER 6

MY HELPFUL FRIENDS ARE NO HELP

"Hey, you never know. Maybe no one will be interested. Then your parents give up on the whole idea, and *you* get a pretty sweet room, right?"

That's Gus's take on what's happened to me.

I am sitting with my two best friends at lunch on the first day of school. Normally we'd be talking about our classes, who we got as teachers, who changed over the summer—you know, the usual stuff. But this AirHotel thing obviously takes priority.

"I wouldn't count on it. You live on a pretty desirable street," says Nat. As usual, she makes more sense than Gus. Nat is short for Natalie. But no one calls her Natalie except teachers and her parents.

Gus takes a bite of his sloppy joe. Unfortunately, over the summer, the cafeteria people (notice I don't call them cooks because I'm pretty sure they didn't cook this stuff—it was made in a lab somewhere for them to reheat and torture kids with) didn't decide to magically improve the quality of the food they serve. Gus doesn't seem to mind. He's already hit his growth spurt. I remember learning in science that hummingbirds have to eat two or three times their body weight daily to live. Someone should tell Gus he's not a hummingbird. He's like five foot nine and his voice is already changing.

Nat digs into her lunch. She never has to eat the school lunch. She brings hers from home. Well, not home exactly. The Haddads have had a store on Atlantic Avenue serving Middle Eastern and other specialty foods for almost a hundred years. So Nat brings in homemade hummus, falafel, and fresh-baked pita. I would be incredibly jealous, except that she always brings enough to share.

She offers me some of the foil-wrapped pita bread, made just this morning. I tear off a piece of the still-warm pita and dip it into the hummus. Like always, the lid is emblazoned with HADDAD'S—SINCE 1905.

Believe me, there is nothing like Haddad's hummus. It's completely different from that junk you get at a grocery store, where all you taste is lemon and garlic. This is smooth, almost sweet, and melts on your tongue.

Gus looks over wistfully. "I wish my dad would let me bring stuff from the store."

Gus's dad owns Baublitz Butcher Shop on Court Street.

They've been there even longer than Nat's family. Both my friends have families that have been in the neighborhood for generations, which I think is kind of cool.

Nat looks at me, her black eyebrows joining together in concentration. "Maybe the AirHotel isn't such a bad thing."

"Four girls—" I start.

"Would you just get off that?" she says, irritated. "It's not going to happen. This is Brooklyn. Think of who is actually going to stay there."

"I dunno. I could get into four girls staying at our house if they were cute enough," says Gus.

"Shut up. You're gross," groans Nat. "You have yucky meat grease all over your face."

Gus wipes his face with a napkin. "I was just trying to make the best of the situation." He brightens. "Here's an idea. When people come to visit, sit on the couch in the living room in your underwear, picking your belly button. They'll be so grossed out, they'll leave bad reviews."

Gus is full of ideas. They're just not usually very good.

"My parents would really appreciate that," I said. "Before they killed me."

Nat harrumphs. "Look, I think you should give this a chance. It's a way to meet people from all sorts of backgrounds and show them the best of Brooklyn."

"But it's just that a promise is a promise," I start. They've heard this a million times from me by now.

"Yeah, it stinks," says Gus, "but you gotta accept it. You know, like I said, make the best of it."

I turn to Nat. "So you really think it could be a good experience?"

She looks me full in the face. I hadn't really noticed how much older she looks now. I guess she had her growth spurt too. She could pass for fourteen, easy. "Yes. I think you should look at this as a real opportunity."

I tear off another piece of pita. "So if it was you, you'd welcome it?"

Nat laughs. "Me? No way. I'd hate it. I'd be furious at my parents."

CHAPTER 7

MOVIE MAGIC

I love walking home after school. It's one of my favorite things about Brooklyn: you can walk places. No waiting around for your parents to pick you up in the minivan. Okay, that's not true. There *are* lots of kids whose parents drive them to soccer practice and dance class and whatever, just like in the suburbs. But most of *my* friends don't do those kinds of things. (It's the private school kids who do.) If we have to go anywhere, we take the subway or bus.

Lucky for me, Nat and Gus moved on to the same middle school. Nat is smart enough that she got into one of those public schools for gifted kids, but she decided to stay in the neighborhood. In her opinion, those kids are stuck-up and think they're better than everybody else. Her parents weren't happy. Their culture puts a lot of importance on getting the best education you can get. Nat told them Jake went to our middle school and got into Cornell, so that made them feel better. I told you she's smart.

Gus and me, we don't really have a choice. I mean, I'm not stupid or anything, but at the same time I'm not one of the smart kids, the ones who get the math problems done in half the time, or figure out that the owl in some short story or poem we read is a symbol of death or something like that. I thought it was just an owl. So sue me.

Anyhow, I'm heading home, and it's one of those early fall days where Brooklyn looks particularly great, especially our neighborhood, where the houses are all small brownstones with stoops and big parlor windows. The sun is putting deep shadows on all the buildings, bringing out the dark reds of the bricks and the dusky greens of the rooftops. Hey, that's not bad. Maybe it symbolizes something.

It's no surprise when a block from my house I get stopped by this young guy in a baseball cap holding a walkie-talkie. I know from experience what's going on.

"Just a minute, bro," he says, holding up a hand to block my way.

I look up the street and see a huge film crew. There's a camera on a crane, director's chairs, a food service truck, and trailers where the actors get their makeup and hair done.

They're doing a take, so I can't cross the street or I'll be in the scene.

Most places, if they're shooting a movie in your neighborhood it would be a big deal, with all the kids and old people hanging around. It would be all anyone talked about for days.

Here, it's just another Monday.

You've probably seen my building in a hundred movies, TV shows, and commercials. It's just so "charming" and such a "typical city street" that someone is shooting something every week, or so it seems.

The crew finishes the take, and the stuck-up PA (which stands for production assistant—you learn these things after the twentieth time one of them acts like a self-important jerk) waves me through. I wander by. The name of the production is written on the backs of the chairs and taped up on the actors' trailers. It's called *Only the Dead Know Brooklyn*.

There's a big burly type with a belt full of tools adjusting a clamp on a tripod holding some sort of lighting. These guys are always the friendliest.

"So what's this one about?" I ask him.

He looks down at me and laughs. "I dunno, kid. Some sort of horror film. I think the place is haunted or something."

Another one of those. "Sounds pretty corny to me," I say.

He tightens a bolt on the tripod with one last twist. "Hey,

as long as the check clears. I don't write 'em, I don't see 'em, I don't even care if it's a flop or wins an Oscar. I just put the stuff up and take it down when they tell me."

Only he doesn't say "stuff." This is Brooklyn, and people aren't always so careful about cursing in front of kids.

CHAPTER 8

RICHIE THE NUMBERS RUNNER
AND OTHER MYSTERIES

I get home and walk up the steps of our stoop to our apartment. Our building is one of the older ones on the block, and it's a lot wider than some of the others. That just means we have to share it with three other renters.

Downstairs is a doctor's office. Dr. Chun is an ophthalmologist, which is handy since all of us wear glasses. She lives in the other apartment on our floor with her husband and baby girl, Gloriana. Their apartment is 2F, since they're in the front. Ours is 2R, because . . . that's obvious, right?

One flight up from us, in the front, is Marjorie, a lady in her thirties who writes for a travel magazine. She's never home. We water her plants all the time. And in the back is an old man named Richie.

Richie's been living here forever. My dad remembers

him as an old man when *he* was a kid. Richie wears an old-fashioned hat with a little snap brim and dresses very nicely, but seems to only go to the corner newspaper store and hang out with some other old guys. My dad swears he's a bookie or a numbers runner. I'm not exactly sure what a numbers runner does, so I looked it up online once and it has to do with people in the neighborhood betting on certain numbers with him, and if the number "comes up," he pays them off. Of course it's totally illegal, but nobody seems to care because it's only old people in our neighborhood who do it.

Richie is real quiet. He's also real old. Like how old, I have no idea. Maybe in his eighties? He never says hello. Just nods when he sees me and goes back to his newspaper.

I get to the front door and since I have my own key, I let myself in.

Having my own key is a big deal, and just started with this school year. I have a bad habit of losing things, so my folks never felt it was a good idea to give me a key. Besides, with dad working at home, it wasn't really an issue. I'd just ring the bell like a thousand times and that would be that. I guess I'm old enough now to be trusted or something, but it's a cool feeling to let yourself in and out of the building.

As soon as I walk into our apartment, I am assaulted with the smell of new paint. I hear running water and the radio blaring music from the bathroom and put two and two together. I head to the back of the apartment and see that Dad hired Gabriel to paint Jake's room while I was at school.

It's now a pale green (I learn later from my mom that the color is called "mint"), and with the Gorillaz and *Pulp Fiction* posters removed from the walls, and the new bed and everything, I barely recognize it.

"Hey, Danilo!" Gabriel calls out. That's his nickname for me. I like it. "Your dad's on a call. Very important. You want to help me? The paint should be dry by now."

I shrug off my backpack and enter Jake's room. As I pass through the doorway I feel that chill again, but it's probably just because I know I'm not getting my wish and someone else is going to be sleeping in *my* room.

We take up the newspaper from the floor and then get to work peeling off the blue painter's tape from all the things Gabriel covered in the room, like the doorknobs and baseboards. I'm finishing up as Gabriel starts to pull the drop cloths off all the new furniture he and my dad assembled over the weekend.

My dad comes in and helps us push everything into position. He helps Gabriel hang the big framed print, and we put some books in the newly painted bookcase. Mom has actually gone to the trouble to pick out what she thinks are books that people would like to look at during their stay, like the big photo book of Brooklyn she gave my dad a few years ago.

We step back and look at the results.

"Not bad," my dad says. "I'd stay here."

"I wish I could," I say, not looking at anyone in particular.

My dad reaches over and rubs my shoulders. "So do I, Danny boy."

"So we all good for now, Mr. Martin?" asks Gabriel.

Dad nods and reaches into his pocket. "It's great. I couldn't have done it without you. What's the damage?"

That's my dad's way of asking "How much do I owe you?"

Bored, I launch myself onto the bed.

The whole thing collapses under me.

CHAPTER 9

THE FACE IN THE WINDOW

My dad and Gabriel have just finished reassembling the bed, both of them insisting that they tightened the screws perfectly the first time.

"It's like someone went around and loosened them right after we finished!" Gabriel says, laughing. "Danilo, you playing tricks?"

I know he's joking, but just to be sure, they check each other's work. This time I sit gingerly on the bed. It holds.

There is the sound of a key in the lock, and Mom's voice calls out, "Hello? Is anyone here?"

It's Mom's "I have someone with me, so nobody say anything stupid" voice, and we hear her talking to someone as she heads toward Jake's room. "Since the room is in the back, it kind of affords our guests privacy."

"Totally, you have to mention that," a young woman's voice answers.

Mom arrives at the room. She's dressed more casually than her usual office clothes, so I'm guessing she's taken time off to meet with this person.

The girl she's with is maybe twenty or maybe older (I'm bad at guessing girls' ages) and has dyed hair and a pierced nose. She's wearing a black leather motorcycle jacket and has a messenger-style bag slung over one shoulder. She looks really familiar. Maybe she works at the fancy chain coffee and pastry shop that's a block from our house. Or maybe she's a nanny.

Gabriel's face brightens when he sees her. "Hey! I know you! You're the nice one! The one who doesn't leave the bags in our garbage."

The girl laughs and bows. "That's me!"

Mom quickly says, "This is Katia. She's been helping me write the description of the bedroom."

Gabriel looks confused. "But I thought—"

"I also walk dogs," Katia says.

So that's how I know her! I see Katia every morning on the way to school with like ten dogs on leashes. It reminds me of that picture book I loved as a kid, *Go, Dog. Go!* Big dogs. Little dogs. Fluffy dogs. Short-haired dogs. You'd think it would be hard for the little ones to keep up with the big ones, but somehow they manage.

"I wish they were all like you," Gabriel mutters. "Those ones who leave the bags . . ."

Katia shoots him a sympathetic look. We all know what he's referring to.

In New York you have to pick up the poop after your dog finishes. And then you have to figure out where to throw it away.

There are always some thoughtless people who think it's cool to throw it in our trash cans, which is gross for Gabriel because, well, do I have to spell it out? It's just gross.

Gabriel checks his cell phone. He does stuff for like ten buildings in the neighborhood and is a really good handyman, so usually someone is trying to find him.

He puts his phone in his pocket and turns to my parents. "Okay, I gotta go. You don't need me for anything else, right?"

"No, it looks fantastic!" my mom exclaims as Gabriel leaves. She turns to Katia with a worried look on her face. "Right?"

As I look around, I realize that the room now looks exactly like those sample rooms I love at the Ikea store. But somehow here in our house it doesn't look as great. It's kind of bland and soulless. Generic. No personality. If it was a person, it would be boring.

But Katia is nodding. "It's perfect. Great job, Maureen."

Katia opens the flap on her messenger bag and takes out a humongous, expensive-looking camera.

"So you're not just a dog walker," I say, stating the obvious.

"Katia got a degree in photography from Eastman," my mother says.

I know I need to say something. "Wow." I have no idea what Eastman is, but I assume it's impressive.

"Yeah, I've been in a few gallery shows," Katia says to me as if I'm someone she needs to impress. "But that's my art. This is to make a living."

She paces around the room.

"So you really think someone would want to stay here?" I ask, hoping she'll say something like "Well, it's only one room, and they have to share a bathroom. . . ."

Instead she says, "Are you kidding? With all this natural light and a garden view? You're going to be booked up in no time."

My mom is glowing.

Katia picks a spot and motions for me to get out of the way. She squats down and clicks off a few shots. She moves around the room, shooting more and more.

My mom leans into me and whispers, "She's already shot the outside of the house and the block. Katia says that's going to be a big selling point, all the charm."

Katia pushes past us to get a few shots of the bathroom

and then comes back into the room. She checks the screen on the back of the camera. Her face scrunches up. She's pressing buttons. She mutters something under her breath.

"Is there something wrong?" my mom asks.

"Yeah. I can't seem to find the images of the bedroom. This is crazy. I mean, I've been checking all along. But they've disappeared."

The hair on my arms stands up. Just the bedroom? That *is* weird.

"Oh, dear," my mom says. "Do you think it's the camera?"

Katia looks annoyed. "I just had this serviced. If it is, I'm going to kill them."

She checks the screen again, scrolling through images. "I don't get it. The ones from outside are all there. And so are the ones of the bathroom and the kitchen. Just the ones of the bedroom are missing."

"But didn't you take a whole bunch of shots in the bathroom *after* the bedroom?" I ask. "It's like the bedroom ones were specifically erased."

No one else seems to find this eerie, just peculiar.

Katia flips a latch at the bottom of the camera and removes the memory card. "It *could* be the memory card, but I've never had this happen before. I'll try another one."

She puts one in, squats down again, and clicks off a few frames. She checks the shots. "Now they're there. This is so random."

She shoots a couple more and looks again. "Yeah, now I got 'em. Let me just check the focus."

She presses a button. "Huh," she says, and laughs. "That's so crazy."

"Don't tell me they're gone again," my mother sighs.

I peer over Katia's shoulder as she zooms in on an image and get another deep chill. "No . . . ," she says. "I guess it's your reflection behind me, Maureen. I wouldn't have even seen it if I hadn't zoomed in."

But the reflection doesn't look like my mom at all.

"Don't worry," Katia is saying, "I can remove it in Photoshop, no problem. We're good."

"What is it?" my mom asks.

"It's . . . well . . ."

I look once more and answer for Katia. "It looks like there's a face in the window. Staring in."

CHAPTER 10

STEEPED IN CHARM

It's Friday afternoon, and the first week of school is over, and I'm hanging out with Gus and Nat. We're sitting on the promenade overlooking the East River. It's one of the best views of the lower Manhattan skyline in the city. It's also got a playground where little kids from all over the neighborhood lose their minds running around and screaming like banshees. This is where the three of us first met all those years ago when our moms would take us here.

"I've already decided that Mr. Sanderson hates me," I say.

Mr. Sanderson is my geometry teacher. He's been at the school like forever, and of course he had Jake when Jake was in sixth grade.

"Which one is Sanderson, again?" Gus asks. He has Mrs.

Tolskaya. She's Russian and really nice, from what everyone says.

"He's the one who kind of stopped paying attention to clothes after the nineties, right?" Nat says.

I crack open a pistachio. "Whenever they stopped wearing those sweaters with patterns so loud they hurt your eyes. Somebody forgot to tell him."

"He also has those huge glasses like my dad has in his wedding pictures," Nat tells Gus. "But now my dad would not be caught dead in them, while I guess Sanderson is waiting for them to come back into fashion."

"So he's a jerk?" Gus asks, getting right to the point. "You figured that out already?"

"You tell me," I say. "I think it was jerky of him to make a big deal about Jake in front of the entire class, and to say, 'If you're half the student your brother was . . . ,' like I have to live up to Jake's reputation or something. He calls on me all the time, and if I get anything wrong, or ask him to explain something again, he sighs and looks all disappointed."

Nat shakes her head. "I think you're being a little oversensitive, Danny."

A kid from our class wanders over. He's a head taller than me and wearing a stained T-shirt with some old rock band's logo on it. He's also wearing enough body spray to fumigate a basketball court.

"You're in my homeroom, right?" he asks Nat, ignoring Gus and me.

"We all are," Nat says evenly.

"So, I was, like, curious. . . ." He smirks, which goes perfectly with his Eau de Madison Square Garden cologne. "You're an Arab, right?"

Gus and I both tense up. This sort of question sucks.

Nat answers with a practiced casualness. "Actually, I'm an American. Of Arab descent, though."

"Oh, that's cool. But, like, how come you're not wearing one of those headscarf things?"

Nat doesn't even blink. I've heard her have this conversation probably a dozen times, even with one or two rude teachers.

"First of all, not all Arabs are Muslim. I'm Christian."

The smelly kid guffaws. "No way! Christian Arabs? That's a real thing?"

"Second of all, even if I was, not all Muslim girls wear headscarves. Just so you know."

It takes a while for this to sink in. He looks perplexed.

Gus is about to step between the kid and Nat but she stops him. "Any other questions?"

There's a moment, and the kid shrugs. "Nah. Just curious, you know?"

"You've got your answer," Gus says, with a "don't push it" edge to his voice.

"All right! Calm down, killer." The Cologne Kid laughs and walks away. "Take it easy. Just askin' a few questions. You people are so sensitive."

Gus looks after him, his fists balled.

I look at Nat. "I'm sorry you get that stuff."

Nat clearly wants to change the subject. "Anyhow, Danny, I think *you're* being overly sensitive about this whole Jake thing."

I want to say, "You know, if I had a nice big room to myself to study in, maybe my grades would be as good as Jake's," but of course, I don't. They've heard me complain about it too much already.

We make plans to meet tomorrow at Brooklyn Bridge Park, and Nat heads home. Gus heads to his father's shop. He helps out on Fridays, making deliveries if they're close or just hanging out and "learning the business," as his father says.

I get home to find my mother in front of her laptop, reading something out loud to my dad.

My dad looks up from his editing. "They both sound great. I don't know." He's barely listening to her. He motions me over. "Look at the comments this mom gave me on her son's bar mitzvah video. 'Not funny enough. Can you film more of his friends saying things about him? I gave you the video of Eli in *The Music Man* where he was so brilliant. Why didn't you use the whole song?'

"If I do what she asks, the video's going to be twenty

minutes at least and nobody is going to watch it," he tells me. "But she's the client, so I have to do it."

Mom looks irritated. "Would you listen to me? Which do you think is better? 'Steeped in Charm: Room in the Heart of Historic Brooklyn Heights' or 'Room in Hottest Brooklyn Neighborhood, Steps Away from the Subway'?"

She turns to me. "Which do you like?"

I remember when Jake used to come home and Mom and Dad would ask how school was. Guess that was then. This is now.

"I like the second one," I say. "But we're not *really* steps from the subway. It's like five blocks away."

My dad doesn't look up from his monitor but says, "Well, technically you're not lying. It *is* steps. Just a whole lot of them."

That makes my mom laugh. "Okay, okay. I need to get to the description."

She reads it like a thousand times and finally calls her brother in Los Angeles to read it to him.

"So, Artie, would you stay here? I mean, if you read it on-line? What? Oh, that's *good*! Thanks, love you!" Mom turns to us, nodding. "He's so smart. He said, 'Put in a sentence about how the hosts know the area and can recommend the best pizza and other Brooklyn delights.' Also, he sent me a link to a map showing where famous writers have lived near here, which we can print out and leave on the bed."

"Of course he did," my dad says.

Uncle Artie is an English professor, so it makes total sense. How many people are going to care is another matter.

My mom takes off her reading glasses and pushes her chair back. She turns the laptop toward me.

The posting is really impressive. Katia's pictures of the neighborhood and the interior make it all look so attractive. And Mom's little paragraph is pretty good, to be honest.

"I'd stay here," I say, trying to be supportive.

My mom beams and hugs me. "Me too."

"Too bad I can't," I add. I can't help myself. She playfully smacks me away.

My dad comes over and wraps his arms around me. "We wish you could too," he says. "And you will. This is only temporary."

"Well, here goes," my mom announces as she clicks the Publish button.

There's a weird flicker on the screen. Then, a message pops up.

We are unable to process your request. For any technical issues, please call or email.

"I did everything right!" my mom exclaims. "I know I did!"

"Try it again," my dad says. "Or let me."

He sits and patiently retypes her beloved paragraph, and uploads all the photos again.

There's a momentary pause as the images load. He clicks Publish.

We are unable to process your request. . . .

The three of us stare at the screen. My mom takes out her phone.

"Funny," my dad says. "You'd think someone put a curse on renting the room or something."

CHAPTER 11

WHISPERING WALLS

It takes my mom most of the rest of the evening to get things sorted out. I do homework in my closet room. I wanted to use the new desk, but I was told that was off-limits, like I was going to get it dirty or something. I would have said something, but Mom was on hold with the tech support guy at AirHotel, and in no mood for smart remarks. That's exactly what she would have said if I had tried to argue.

My mom started out with the guy using her nice professional voice, one grown-up to another. But now she's losing it.

"Yes, of course I went to the troubleshooting page on your website first," I hear her say, her voice rising. "If that worked would I be talking to you?"

She shoots a look at my dad and puts the phone on speaker

so Dad can hear. The tech support guy has a chirpy voice. He's happy to help. And apparently clueless.

My dad takes over, and escalates the call to the next-level technician. He's really good talking to these phone people. It doesn't matter if it's our cell phone provider or the cable or health insurance company.

Dad can get what he wants.

My mom looks at him gratefully. Her hero.

After more cheesy jazz music, a person comes on who sounds like he's had fewer cups of coffee and knows a little more. He and Dad try to figure out if it's the antivirus software on the computer, or maybe an issue with the browser. I keep thinking of Dad's words. Maybe the room doesn't want to be rented.

Ultimately, my dad has to send the files to the guy so *he* can upload them onto the site. My mom is asking questions like "Are you sure this is going to work?" Which is never helpful.

My dad doesn't even bother to answer, just does what he's told, and then they have to wait for the files to show up. The guy on the phone, Alex (Dad, the pro, gets his name and uses it every other sentence: "Great, *Alex*. We couldn't have done it without you, *Alex*. Of course I'm going to fill out the survey at the end of the call, *Alex*."), tells Dad that he'll get the files up tomorrow morning and they should be able to see their submission by the afternoon.

Alex then adds, "Glad I could help. And this one was new to me. I've been doing this for four years and this is the first time I've ever come across this. I really can't explain why we couldn't get it to go through."

They say their goodbyes, and my mom tackles my dad and hugs him. She does this whenever he saves her from some situation she would never have gotten through herself.

My mom gives my dad one more hug and looks at the screen hopefully.

"He said tomorrow," my dad says gently.

"I know. I can't help it. I can't wait," Mom says.

It's past my bedtime. I need to get up tomorrow for school, so I say my goodnights and close the door.

•‹ ‹ ‹ ‹3+

At I-don't-know-what in the morning, I get up to pee. I'm about to head back to my room, when I see a light at the end of the hallway.

The door to Jake's room is closed, but there's a faint light showing under the door. Like someone's in there. But it's the middle of the night. I know it's probably just Mom, or that someone left the light on, but something feels weird and I can't just go back to bed.

I want to head to my bedroom, but I find myself walking toward Jake's room. It's not like I made a decision. It's like

49

something is pulling me there. Or someone. I get to the door and reach for the doorknob.

Before I can get to it, it turns by itself.

I watch the knob turn, and then the door slowly opens. There's no one on the other side of it. I can feel my heart pounding under my T-shirt.

I know I should run back to my room, but I'm rooted in place. This is *not* normal. The room is kind of glowing. I go to the window and look out.

No moon. No streetlight. Nothing. Where is the light coming from?

It's as if the room is shining from within, casting black shadows against the walls.

I am trying to breathe normally, but I'm having a hard time.

I want to back out of the room, but something is keeping me frozen to the spot.

That's when I hear the voices in the walls.

I need to interject that hearing things in the walls of an old house like ours is not unusual. You hear running water going through the pipes, arguments between people in apartments next to yours, or loud parties. In my closet, I even hear mice scratching around, which is kind of gross, except it's a lot better than when one of them dies in there. Trust me.

All I'm saying is that hearing things in walls is nothing new. But this is different. It's like the walls themselves are whispering. I can't explain it better than that. It's like the wind, only inside the room. I can't make out what the voices are saying. It's like a moaning.

I begin to shake.

Little by little, the moaning begins to form sounds . . . syllables whispered urgently right into my ear.

"Yaaaah . . . naaaa . . . kella."

The voices keep repeating this over and over again.

They're getting louder and louder and louder. . . .

And then, at the window.

A face appears, pale and angry.

Its eyes are boring right through me, filled with rage.

Another voice surfaces, calling me from far away. "Danny! Danny!"

Then the voice is right next to me.

"Danny!" I startle, and realize I'm in bed, looking at my mother.

CHAPTER 12

NAT IS NOT IMPRESSED

"That is the freakiest thing I have ever heard." Gus's eyes are as big as the falafel balls we got at Haddad's to eat in Brooklyn Bridge Park.

"So what did your parents say?" Gus asks, taking another bite of his pita sandwich. I guess my story didn't do anything to his appetite.

"They just said I had a bad dream and they know that change is hard but I'm going to have to accept it."

This place used to be an eyesore of old warehouses and rotting piers. Back during World War II, many of the great battleships were built right here by the immigrants who had moved to Brooklyn, some of them to escape the very war they were helping end. But after the war, all the shipbuilding moved away and the place just sat here, ugly and unloved (like that kid with the cologne—sorry, he *really* bugged me). Now it's this amazing park, with everything from a barbecue area to volleyball courts, soccer fields, and the piers are walkways leading right out to the water, where you can sit on benches and get an impressive view of Manhattan.

Like I said, normally this is one of my favorite places in the world (okay, I haven't been many places, but you know what I mean), but today everything feels dark and strange, like I can't shake that angry face from my dream.

Nat hasn't said a word. She's just staring at me with her big dark eyes. It's a little unnerving.

I'm dying for her to say something. She reads a lot, so maybe she's read some ghost story that's like this.

"I cannot believe some stupid dream is creeping you out so much," she finally says, rolling her eyes.

I can take anything but the eye roll.

"Look, it didn't feel like it was a dream. It felt real."

Nat looks out over the water. "Duh. I had a dream that I was taking the history midterm in my underwear and it totally felt real."

"This is different," I insist.

"Danny, you've been telling us for a week now how mad you are at your parents for doing this. Clearly this is just your subconscious telling the same story."

I can hear my voice rising. "Oh, really? Then how do you explain the face in the window in those photos? Or the fact that my mom couldn't upload the photos to the AirHotel site?"

Nat is trying hard not to smile, which makes me madder. "You told us yourself the face was probably your reflection," she says. "And really? You think your mom's laptop is haunted? Like you've never had trouble with a computer?"

"So that's your explanation?" I ask.

"Danny, what if this hadn't happened to you?" Nat says. "What if you had heard about someone who really didn't want his parents to rent out his brother's room, and he passes a film crew on the street shooting some ghost story, and then some totally normal things happened that seemed weird because life is sometimes weird, you know."

"My uncle Vince once saw the Virgin Mary on a piece of veal," offers Gus.

"Which applies to this how?" I ask.

"Nat just said life is weird," he answers.

"And sometimes we see things we want to see," Nat adds.

"So you think it's all in my head," I mutter.

"I'm just saying there's an explanation for it, that's all."

"Seriously? You wouldn't say that if it happened to you."

Gus reaches into his bag. "Anyone want some pastrami?"

Mom told me when she was studying to be a social worker

she was trained in conflict resolution. This is Gus's "go-to" for conflict resolution when things get tense. Offer food.

Nat and I stare at him.

"It's the good stuff. The one we make right in the store," he explains. "Normally my dad tells me it's for the customers, but Nellie was the slicer today, so . . ."

Nellie is always sweet to Gus and sneaks him "the good stuff." She's like twentysomething and wants to be a novelist, but thinks it's cool to work at a butcher's. For "life experience," as she puts it.

I take two slices of pastrami, thin as paper. I offer one to Nat as a peace offering. She takes it.

"Hey!" Gus adds, chewing happily. "You know what I just learned from my dad? You'll never guess what part of the cow pastrami comes from."

Nat freezes just as she's about to put her slice in her mouth. "Please don't tell me it's something gross."

"It's cool!" Gus exclaims. "It's made from beef navel! You're actually eating a cow's belly button!"

Nat's face turns green, and she hands Gus back the pastrami.

He shrugs and eats it. "Hey, what matters is how it tastes, right?"

The tension is officially broken, and I put the other slice in my mouth. Gus is right. It's really good. I feel the sun on my face and the sounds of little kids yelling in the playground behind us. I look out at the boats in the harbor. It's all so normal. Could Nat be right? Was it all in my head?

"Danny, just think about it," she says. "Let's say you're right. And the room is haunted. Why did these things start now? Isn't that kind of a coincidence?"

I have no answer for that.

CHAPTER 13

DAAN AND LUUK

I come home to find Mom standing, hands on hips, staring at her laptop screen. Of course it's open to the AirHotel page with our listing. No one has booked the room yet, and she seems to think that refreshing the page every ten seconds will make a difference.

Dad is out, having lunch with his friend the producer.

Jack Tempkin produced an independent film way back in the nineties that got a lot of attention and even an Oscar nomination.

Jack has been one of Dad's biggest fans since he sat on a jury for a competition that Dad's student film was entered into. He's always said Dad's film should have won, and has done everything he can to help raise money so Dad can finally make a real movie.

I like Uncle Jack. He looks like you'd think a producer would look. He's a little guy with a big head, and what hair he has left is combed back. He smokes cigars (not in our house, of course—Mom would kill him) and drinks wine and always has a script under his arm. But his clothes are kind of shabby (he's been wearing the same blazer since I can remember) and his stories are always about giving this person or that person their big break and how they never remember, the ingrates.

It seems that since his big film, none of Uncle Jack's projects have gotten made. But he's always having meetings and is convinced that *this* one is going to be the one to put him "back in the game," as he likes to say. Then he'll be able to bring Dad's movie "to any studio in Hollywood."

Whenever Dad comes back from one of these lunches, he's filled with energy and ideas. It's hard to watch him tell Mom all about Jack's new project, because as much as Mom wants to be supportive, I can tell that she thinks Uncle Jack is just getting Dad's hopes up. It's not that he's lying to Dad, Mom explained to me once. He really believes it. It's just that . . . life doesn't always work out the way you want it.

Tell me about it.

So part of me feels bad that things aren't working out for Mom, and part of me is pretty stoked because I know that after a while, if we get no takers, I can move into the room. I bet I wouldn't have those bad dreams then.

"Do you think I should change the description?" Mom asks me for like the hundredth time. She's already changed it five times and it's only been up for a few days.

"Mom, you have to give it time," I answer. "Besides, anyone staying in Brooklyn now would have booked months ago, wouldn't they?"

Mom sighs. "I guess so. I just thought . . ." She refreshes the page again. I wish she wouldn't do that.

There's the sound of a key in the lock and Dad comes in. The look on his face says that he has news but he's not going to tell Mom unless she asks.

"So how's Jack?" she says.

My dad hangs up his jacket and scarf. "He's great, actually. He thinks NYU is going to offer him a permanent job in the spring."

Usually Dad wears a sweatshirt and jeans around the house. The only time he dresses in what he calls "grown-up clothes" is when he's meeting with a client or going out for lunch with Jack. I guess it makes him feel more like he has a real job or something.

"That's great!" my mom says, and it sounds like she means it. "I bet he's an amazing teacher."

"Apparently they really love him, and want him to do it full time," my dad says, but he doesn't sound happy.

"That's a good thing, right?" I ask.

My dad goes to the fridge and gets some grapes. "Yeah, of course. It's just that—"

"If he takes the job, he wouldn't have time to produce movies," my mom says, finishing his sentence.

Dad's voice sounds a little tight. "Not for a little while. Until he gets settled in. That's what he said."

I can tell my mom is trying hard to sound positive. Dad gets really sensitive about this. "But that doesn't mean he won't eventually be able to help you," she says.

"There are a lot of big names on that faculty," Dad mutters. "He's going to show them my script."

My mom sighs. "That's great. I was just trying to be supportive."

My dad's shoulders slump. "Wasn't I supportive when you wanted to try this AirHotel thing?"

Mom paces back to her laptop and plops down.

I can't take any more of this. I'm about to head to my room when Mom screams.

I should mention here that Mom is a screamer, so this didn't freak me out too much.

Some moms drop a plate and say a curse word (unless they're my aunt Amanda, who has never said anything stronger than "For heaven's sake!" Like she's in a movie or something. She's hilarious). My mother screams.

If she's pouring a glass of water and some splashes over the glass, she screams.

Growing up, I learned to interpret different screams:

"Oops!" (Short, high-pitched.)

"I got a paper cut!" (More like *ow!* But still a scream.)

"There is a dead mouse under my desk!" (Very loud and long.)

This scream was the "something amazing has just happened" scream. She's balled her hands into fists and is punching the air. "Yes! Yes!"

No.

No.

I know exactly what's happened.

Dad and I join her at the screen.

There is a message. "You have a request to book your room! Please read."

Mom breathlessly clicks on the message.

Hallo from Daan and Luuk! We are a couple from the Netherlands who wish to stay at your room. Is it available this weekend?

My mom's hands are practically shaking as she grabs the mouse (the computer one, as opposed to a dead one under her desk. I just want to make that clear because of what I said before). It skitters off the table and she grabs for it.

"Maureen, relax," my dad says, laughing. "They're not going anywhere."

"You don't know that," my mom says. She frantically writes them back. And then sits there, biting her thumb.

There is a *ping* and either Daan or Luuk answers. We go to their profile. It shows a tulip. No photo. But they have amazing reviews from the other people who've hosted them.

It looks like we're going to have company this weekend.

CHAPTER 14

THE ENCHANTED HUMMUS

After texting back and forth, we learn that our guests usually stay at a more expensive AirHotel in Manhattan, but the hosts canceled on them at the last minute. They were desperate for a new place, and thought our room and neighborhood looked charming.

My mom has dusted the entire apartment like twenty times and checked to make sure there's enough toilet paper in the bathroom.

"I just think they're going to be neat," she tells my dad. "We really want a good review from them."

She has convinced him to wear his grown-up clothes, which makes this look kind of weird. I mean, she even got cut flowers from the deli and put them in a vase.

We never have flowers in the house. It looks like someone

else's apartment. Mom has gotten a text from Daan saying they're on their way here from the airport.

There's kind of a feeling like we're waiting for a play to begin. Nobody does anything they normally would do. I check my phone and text Nat and Gus to see if they're around and want to get together later.

The doorbell rings, and Mom lets out a scream (I wonder if I should warn Luuk and Daan). She rushes to the door and flings it open.

Two well-dressed middle-aged men sweep into the apartment.

One is small and slender, and in an expensive-looking bright-red sweater. He's wearing jeans, which also probably cost a fortune and look like someone ironed them. He's wearing black loafers that go perfectly with everything else. He immediately hugs my mother and introduces himself as Daan.

Luuk laughs and shakes my father's hand. "We're Dutch. Maybe you prefer to shake hands, yes?" Luuk is tall and round, and has a scarf wrapped around his neck and tucked into a perfectly fitted white shirt. If any grown-up I knew in Brooklyn tried this, they'd look ridiculous (unless they were like twenty years old, maybe? Nope. They'd still look ridiculous).

But somehow it looks charming on Luuk. Just like his accent.

"And this is our son Daniel," my mother says, awkwardly gesturing to me.

"So pleased to meet you," Luuk says.

"We're going to be sharing a bathroom, is that right?" asks Daan.

I nod, not knowing what to say.

"We shall try not to spend *too* much time there," promises Luuk.

"Unless we eat the wrong things!" says Daan, laughing. "Then, as you say, all bets are off!"

We all laugh at this. I guess Dutch people like bathroom humor. I decide Daan would fit in very well in middle school.

They have matching sets of luggage, made of leather (who has leather luggage?).

Luuk tells us they're here for a few days for a conference. He's a professor of art history at Utrecht University and is giving a talk at the Metropolitan Museum on Sunday.

My mom has gotten hummus from Haddad's and cut pita up into small triangles and toasted them. By now, Daan has joined us at the table. This hummus is our secret weapon.

Daan dips a piece of pita in the hummus and tastes it. His eyes widen and then close. Either he's in ecstasy or he's allergic to sesame seeds.

"You *have* to try this, Luuk! It's *enchanting*."

"I was planning on it," Luuk says, chuckling. He takes a bite and nods.

"This is absolutely the *best* hummus I have ever had!" declares Daan.

"It reminds me of the kind we had in Israel," Luuk says. "You've been, yes?"

"Um, actually no," my dad admits. It's hard to explain to world travelers that we've never been outside the United States.

"But this is *better*," Daan insists. "It must be local."

"The place makes it fresh every day," I tell them. "My friend's family owns it."

Luuk looks over at me. He smiles. "You must take us to their shop before we leave, Daniel."

"I'm so happy to be here! We almost didn't book it," Daan says.

My mother's face turns white. "Why? Was there something wrong with the listing?"

"Yes, your place is a pigsty," says Daan.

My mom looks like she's going to cry.

Luuk pushes Daan. "He's teasing. Look, you've made her upset."

Daan hugs my mom. "I'm so sorry. Your apartment is lovely. It's enchanting."

"It goes well with the hummus," Luuk says, grinning.

"So what was the problem?" my dad asks.

"I don't know," Luuk says. "We tried to book the room three times online. It just wouldn't take our reservation."

I feel a prickle on my neck. Can't wait to tell Nat about *this*.

Daan grabs my mom's hand "But we loved it so much, we

emailed support and they booked it for us. Once they took our credit card, everything started to work fine."

"We thought you should know, in case it happens again," Luuk says.

Daan checks his fancy wristwatch. "Ah, look at the time. We need to meet some friends. Please excuse us."

Luuk smiles at me. "Don't forget, you're taking us to that shop before we leave."

They head back to Jake's room. I guess it's not Jake's room anymore. For the next few days, it's theirs.

My mother fans herself. I turn to my dad. "What's up with her?"

"She's a sucker for European charm," he says.

"They are pretty charming," I say.

My dad nods. "And did you check out that matching luggage?"

CHAPTER 15

WHO'S THERE?

Daan and Luuk have gotten tickets to see a Broadway show and are eating dinner with friends. My mom gives them a spare key.

"Enjoy the show!" my mom says as they are leaving.

"You have seen it, yes? Is it any good?" asks Luuk.

My mom's smile is frozen on her face. "Actually, we haven't . . . gotten to it yet."

Right. The tickets are like four hundred dollars each. Nobody we know goes to Broadway shows. Except maybe on school trips.

I mean, there are *lots* of people in our neighborhood who go, but those are the ones who send their kids to private schools.

The ones who travel to Europe during school break.

The ones who seem to belong in our neighborhood more than we do.

So, maybe I should explain how come we're able to live here?

It helps that my grandparents first rented this apartment in the early sixties, when *no one* wanted to live here. Well, by no one, I mean no young families. They were moving to Long Island, or maybe Westchester, where there were nice schools and it was "safe."

Funny to think about that today, that this was once considered an "unsafe" neighborhood.

I guess it was, kind of. My dad was mugged by other kids on the way to school. There was graffiti everywhere and, from what he tells me, there were a lot more drugs.

But there were also writers and artists and political activists who could afford to live in the apartments that used to be flophouses and rooming houses for the sailors from the boats and the workmen who built them.

Little by little, more people like my grandparents started moving in and deciding to stay, even through the bad years of the eighties. Mr. Nordstrom (our history teacher, in case you forgot) showed us headlines from that time when the rest of the country couldn't have cared less if New York went bankrupt. They saw it as a relic, a fossil. And Brooklyn was still a place you moved *from,* not to.

When my parents got married, they lived in the city, but then my grandparents decided to move upstate.

We have this thing in New York called rent control, which means the landlord can't raise the rent too high as long as your name is on the lease and you don't want to move out. So my parents couldn't pass up a deal like this and took over the apartment. It was still a pretty sketchy neighborhood then, so the owner was happy to have them.

Well, as the years went on, Brooklyn got better and better, and people started to *want* to live here. So the other rents in our building started going higher and higher, and our landlord wasn't so happy about my parents.

He still isn't, but he's *really* unhappy about Richie. Richie has lived here since forever, and isn't going anywhere. He probably pays half what my parents pay.

So now the only people who can afford to live in this part of Brooklyn are either people like Nat and Gus, whose families have been here for generations, or rich bankers, doctors, and lawyers.

It's kind of weird to live in a place you can't afford. It's like pretending we're something we're not.

Luuk sees the look on my mom's face. I can tell he's a really sensitive person by the way he says, "Oh, I know how that is. Only tourists go to Broadway, right? That's how we are in Holland about the windmills!" And then he laughs as he and Daan head out.

Dinner is all about Daan and Luuk, of course. My mom is in love with their sophistication and charm, which she attributes to their being European.

"I think that's more of a gay thing," my dad says.

My mom looks at him sharply. "Are you saying all gay men are sophisticated and charming? That's kind of stereotyping, isn't it?"

"What? I didn't think I was being so prejudiced," my dad protests. "I was trying to pay them a compliment."

I decide to join in. "Yeah, but it's like saying all Jewish people are rich."

"Okay, you're right. I apologize to the gay community," my dad says. "I'm sure there are some sloppy, rude, uncultured gay men out there."

"Please don't bring this up with them," my mother begs.

My dad almost spits out his salad. "Do you *really* think I would do that?"

"No, but my mother would," Mom says. And they both laugh.

I laugh too. My bubbe Ruth (which is what I call my grandmother) is one of those people with no filter. She just says whatever she's thinking. Like she'll greet her son-in-law with "Look at you! What happened? When did you get that belly? You need to get to the gym." Or to me, "Such nice skin he has! Well, he'll probably break out in acne once he hits puberty. You haven't yet, have you, darling?"

So it's a good thing she's not here. Who knows what she'd be asking Luuk and Daan.

"It's so funny, all those extra vowels," Dad says, moving on. "You know Curt, right?"

Mom thinks. "The sound guy, right?"

Curt is responsible for the microphone and checks the sound levels when my dad makes his videos.

"He's Serbian, and his name is actually spelled C–R–T!" my dad exclaims. "I learned that when I wrote his check. He told me there are all sorts of Serbian words that have no vowels at all!"

"Okay," says my mom as I get up to help her clear the table. "Where is this going?"

"I just thought that maybe there could be a trade agreement between Holland and Serbia where they send them their extra vowels since they have a surplus," my dad says, ducking the napkin my mom throws at him.

After all the dishes are put away, I head to my room to finish my homework.

Later, as I fall asleep, I have to admit to myself that having Daan and Luuk here is kind of neat after all.

⊷< < <⅜+

Sometime later, I'm awakened by someone knocking on my door.

Probably Daan or Luuk looking for the bathroom.

But the rapping continues, weirdly insistent. I don't lock my door, so I wonder why they don't just walk in, although it's creepy enough that I'm glad they don't.

Finally, I open the door.

There's no one there.

I look down the hall. Maybe whoever knocked on the door realized his mistake and went to the bathroom?

I head to the bathroom, and it's open. And dark. No one is there. The apartment is quiet. Everyone is sleeping.

It must have been something outside, I decide.

I just *thought* it was a knock on my door.

I close my door, and get back under the covers.

My breathing is finally returning to normal and I'm about to drop off. . . .

There is a knock on my door.

CHAPTER 16

THE ULTIMATE MALTED MILK BALL

Daan swears that he was fast asleep when I heard the knocking. We're at breakfast and Luuk is glaring at him. They are in *matching* robes. I have never seen anyone wear a robe to breakfast before. Clearly Mom hasn't either. She is dazzled by this. She asks if they are silk, and Daan laughs and says, "What else?"

They are having toast and fancy jam that my mom picked up at Haddad's. They have all kinds of imported stuff there. She's never bought it for *us*, of course. But for our guests, nothing is too good.

Luuk takes a bite of toast and a sip of gourmet coffee (also from—well, you know by now). "Daan, you are terrible, scaring the boy like that. This coffee is fantastic, Maureen!"

"You know full well I never left the room last night!" Daan protests.

"I know no such thing." Luuk sniffs. "And you like pulling pranks."

"It's fine, right, Danny?" Dad asks.

"Sure," I say. "I mean, I was a little freaked out, what with all that's been going on with the room—"

My mom cuts me off sharply. "Don't bother them with all that, please."

But of course Luuk and Daan want to hear all about it.

"My family home in Rotterdam was haunted," Daan insists.

Luuk chuckles. "Not this again. Daan hears the china rattling in the cabinet and insists it's his grandmother, coming back to make sure he doesn't chip any of it."

Daan looks at me. "They don't believe us. Well, I think it's fascinating. Do you think it's your grandmother?"

Dad is going to fall out of his chair, he's laughing so hard. "Luckily both of Danny's grandmothers are alive. And if my mother-in-law could haunt us after death, she'd be doing a lot worse than knocking on doors!"

"As a matter of fact, I don't remember my mom ever knocking on a door before she came in!" my mom adds, grasping my dad's arm and joining in the hysteria.

Daan raises his eyebrows. "That must have made for an interesting adolescence!"

The whole table is laughing now. Except me. I kind of think I know what Daan is talking about, but I'm not sure, and my cluelessness makes the whole thing even funnier to them.

"You are terrible, Daan," Luuk says, wiping his eyes. "You owe Danny an apology."

Daan bows in my direction. "Please accept my apologies, Dan-with-one-a."

I get up to clear everyone's plates. As soon as my back is turned they all start laughing again. Being thirteen really stinks.

Luuk's conference is in the evening, so it's decided I'll bring them over to Haddad's this morning. I text Gus and Nat to meet me there.

We walk the tree-lined streets and Daan remarks on how it reminds him of parts of Amsterdam, although the houses here aren't nearly as old. He pulls up some pictures on his phone to show me.

"They're beautiful," I say.

"Perhaps you can come and visit Holland with your folks on your summer holiday," Luuk says.

I look away. "I don't think so. We really have to save money for Jake's college. . . ."

"And what about your college?" Luuk asks gently. I realize that his eyes are like the kindest I've ever seen.

I shrug. "I guess we're focusing on Jake right now."

"That doesn't seem fair," Daan says.

"Perhaps we shouldn't be talking about this," Luuk suggests.

"That's okay," I insist. "I'm used to it. Really. It's fine."

Haddad's. It takes up three storefronts, with its name emblazoned in big letters over each. There are displays in every window, with goods from around the world stacked in cool little groups. Setting them up is usually Nat's job, as she's small and can fit into the windows easily to move things around.

Across Atlantic Avenue there are other Middle Eastern stores. Unlike Haddad's, they cater mostly to the Arabs who have been living here forever. They carry a lot of the same spices and nuts and stuff that Haddad's does, but there are hookahs (those water pipes you sometimes see in old movies) and ornamental swords in their windows too. There are entire stores dedicated to Muslim women's fashion, with beautiful hijabs (the headscarves that rude kid was asking Nat about) in all styles and colors. There's a travel agency specializing in Middle Eastern trips, a translation service, and a bakery that has delicacies even Haddad's doesn't carry.

On the street, gray-bearded men in long caftans fingering worry beads gather in groups while kids run around their legs.

But Haddad's is different. It is geared more to the whole neighborhood, and has always embraced the latest food trends. As we walk in the door, I smell the familiar scent of fresh coffee, spices, and the food counter where we get our hummus and other delicacies. Shelf after shelf is lined with anything you might want, like cheeses from France, Spain, Greece, and Switzerland and five types of English mustard (four wasn't enough?).

Nat waves from the other side of the store, in the section with large plastic containers of nuts and dried fruits and candies. I bring Luuk and Daan over to introduce them.

"This is my friend Natalie. It's her family's store."

Luuk shakes her hand. "We are dazzled."

Daan grabs her other hand. "We *must* sample everything!"

Nat laughs. "That's going to be hard."

The two men go off to decide what they want to buy, and I tell Nat what happened last night.

"You were dreaming again," she says simply.

"I was not. I was wide awake."

"You *thought* you were awake."

Now I'm getting mad. "I *know* I was awake. You weren't there."

Nat puts on a plastic glove and reaches into a huge jar labeled ULTIMATE MALTED MILK BALLS. She knows these are my favorites. They are practically as big as tennis balls and filled with milk chocolate, like a regular malted milk ball but on steroids. It's totally a peace offering.

Of course, just as she hands it to me, a voice says, "Oh, great. None for me?"

Nat sighs and hands hers to Gus, who's just arrived.

He looks at her. "Are you sure about this?"

Nat says simply, "I don't need it."

"Well, I don't *need* it either," says Gus, popping the whole thing in his mouth. Which is as gross as it sounds.

That's the moment Luuk and Daan come back. I try to introduce Gus, who cannot speak coherently with the giant malted milk ball in his mouth. He pushes it over to one cheek, which makes him look a little like a demented hamster.

Luuk pretends not to notice.

Daan nods. "Are those the ultimate malted milk balls?" He scribbles them on their list.

A woman behind the counter gestures to Luuk and Daan.

"We're next!" says Luuk, and rushes off.

I tell Gus about the knocking. His eyes widen.

"Dude, I've seen this movie." (The candy has melted enough for me to make out what he's saying.) "If it was me, I'd get out of there and never look back."

CHAPTER 17

THIRTY-SEVEN DIFFERENT TYPES OF OLIVES

The fact that someone else has finally said what I've been thinking hits me a lot harder than I thought it would. I'm finding it hard to catch my breath. I can feel a dampness under my arms.

Nat must have noticed that I've broken out in a sweat.

"First of all," she says, pushing Gus in the chest, "it's not a haunted house. It's an apartment. And it sounds like only one room is haunted."

I look at her.

"I mean, *if* it was actually haunted," she adds quickly, "which it isn't. Because ghosts aren't real."

"I dunno," Gus says. "I saw this special on the History Channel where they brought all this equipment into a haunted castle and they were scientists and everything. They couldn't explain what they were finding."

"Those shows are all fake," Nat snorts. "I'd like to know what sort of scientists they were."

"All I know is they were wearing white coats," Gus insists. "And it was on the History Channel, not Syfy."

I sigh. "Gus, the History Channel also has those pawnshop shows where people just happen to show up with incredibly valuable things they found in their garage. It's all scripted."

"It *is*?" Gus whimpers. "I always thought—"

"Everybody knows all those shows are hyped," Nat adds. "*Especially* the ones that claim to prove ghosts are real."

It always calms me down when Nat argues, because she's so persuasive. At school, she's the one who makes the best points about the books we're reading. Right now, I want to believe that she's right. I mean, it just isn't logical. Right?

"What about the knocking?" Gus persists. "How do you explain that?"

Nat reaches into the jar and offers Gus another malted milk ball. "Just because we don't know why Danny heard what he did doesn't mean there isn't a logical explanation."

The malted milk ball has temporarily distracted Gus as Nat knew it would. Just then Daan and Luuk come up, their basket filled to overflowing with bags of dried fruits, candies, and some of the prepared foods from the deli section.

"These are some of the best stuffed grape leaves I've ever had!" exclaims Luuk, licking his fingers.

"Just *some* of the best?" a booming voice demands. "I'm disappointed! Usually people say they are *the* best they've ever had!"

I smile when I see the imposing form of Sammy Haddad, Nat's grandfather. Whenever I see the word "jolly" in a book, I think of him. It's hard not to.

He's impossible to miss. He's over six feet tall, with a big strong chest and a belly to match, usually under a brightly checked shirt. I don't know if I've ever seen him frown except when he's pretending to be mad or acting exasperated because a customer hasn't found the cheese he's given her to taste "the best she's ever had."

Sammy has been the face of Haddad's since he was Nat's age, probably.

My dad likes to talk about having "people skills," meaning the ability to talk to people and make them feel at ease or charmed. Usually when he's talking about it, it's in the negative ("That kid's mother is severely lacking in people skills"). But I think Sammy might have invented people skills. He's talking to Luuk and Daan like they're old friends. The way he's shaking both their hands you'd think they were buying thousands of dollars' worth of food.

"If you treat your new customers like this, I can't imagine how you treat your old ones!" Daan says. "I feel like family!"

Sammy leans down to them conspiratorially. "I treat my old customers *better* than family. Some of my family I don't like so much. I love all my customers!"

This is followed by his trademark laugh, which is so deep, it seems to come from all over his body.

Sammy has known so many of us since we were babies, and he remembers everyone's name.

Luuk, who is pretty good in the people skills department himself, is about to charmingly answer him when someone calls for Sammy.

"Please excuse me," Sammy says. "I'll be right back! Be good! And if you can't be good, be careful!"

Another laugh, which we can't help but join in, as corny as Sammy is. He's got signs all over the store saying things like YOU DON'T HAVE TO BE CRAZY TO WORK HERE . . . BUT IT HELPS! And A WAIST IS A TERRIBLE THING TO MIND!

The thing is, he really thinks the signs are funny. As he passes, a dad holding a baby yells, "Why can't I be more like you, Sammy? You get so much joy out of life."

Sammy answers, "You want to be more like me? An overweight old guy with glasses and bad feet? I'd rather be a handsome young man like you, but I'm stuck with what I've got, so I might as well make the best of it!"

The customer who asked for him has come back to the neighborhood for a visit and of course *had* to buy something at Haddad's. This happens all the time. The people want to reminisce, talk about all the changes in Brooklyn, and just let Sammy know how happy they are that no matter what, Haddad's is still here.

Sammy looks into the stroller. "Don't tell me this gorgeous creature is your granddaughter?"

"Yes, this is Paloma," the white-haired woman says.

"Please. You're far too young to have grandchildren."

The woman shakes her head, laughing. "Oh, Sammy, you're too much!"

"I know!" Sammy says. "My doctor says I need to lose thirty pounds!"

They hug, and he returns to us.

"Lovely people," he says. "Used to live around the block years ago."

To be honest, Sammy thinks all of his customers are lovely people. Although it's funny, because he doesn't run the store anymore; his kids do. Not that he made them do it. Sammy is very proud that he didn't force his kids to go into the business. Both his daughter, Marie (Nat's mom), and his son, Michael, went to college and business school because they *wanted* to take over the family business one day. Of course, that doesn't stop Sammy from coming in every morning and acting like he still runs things.

He turns to Daan and Luuk. "I thought I heard an accent. I'm guessing . . . you're Dutch?"

"Very good!" Daan says, beaming.

"We carry Vanderdonk chocolates, the best in Amsterdam, yes?" Sammy says, not waiting for an answer. "And of course, when it comes to Edam . . . ," Sammy calls out to the woman at the cheese counter. "How many cheeses do we have from Holland?"

"Six or seven," she reports.

"But of course you don't want that!" Sammy says, laughing. "You can get that any time at home!" He checks their basket. "Hmm . . . good, good. But wait!"

Nat is grinning and gives me a look. I mouth the words "Thirty-seven types of olives," and she giggles. It's only a matter of time before Sammy mentions his pride and joy. "No olives?"

Luuk and Daan exchange glances.

Daan bows. "We were overwhelmed with the choices!"

Sammy has led them over to a rectangular chrome showpiece holding canister after canister of gleaming olives.

"I don't blame you! We have . . ." Sammy pauses, beaming. Here it comes. "*Thirty-seven* different types of olives! You can't walk out of here without trying some of them!"

Ten minutes later, having been subjected to a lecture on the differences between kalamata and Greek olives, and having sampled more than a dozen, Luuk and Daan have made their decision. They look a little overwhelmed.

Sammy has that effect on a lot of people.

As they head to the cash register, Sammy turns to us and

makes sure we try his newest batch of olives from the South of France.

Sammy tells us they are "right off the boat!"

They are delicious, but I'm not sure I could tell the difference.

"So what are you young people up to today?" he asks.

Before I can stop him, Gus says, "We were just talking about how Danny's apartment is haunted."

I thought Sammy would laugh like he always does, but instead he rubs his chin.

"Haunted, you say? That's serious business. Tell me about it."

CHAPTER 18

YOU DON'T KNOW WHAT YOU DON'T KNOW

Nat looks like she's going to explode. *"Jidoo!"* That's the Lebanese word for grandpa. "This is one of your jokes, right?"

Sammy looks down at her. "You know, Nat, not everything is a joke."

"Please. I can't believe you are serious!"

Sammy looks pretty serious, though. "Look, if it was Gus, I'd just laugh, because Gus is a prankster."

Gus looks a little hurt, but also a little proud.

Sammy looks over at me. "But this is Danny. He's a very sensible boy."

Nat snorts. She's seen me in the lunchroom.

Sammy shrugs. "I mean, as thirteen-year-old boys go. He doesn't make stuff up."

"I guess that's true," Nat admits.

There is an older couple by the registers. They see Sammy and wave. He waves back and yells, "Good to see you again!"

He gestures to us to follow him. "Too many distractions out here. Come, come, come." He leads us to a small office in the back of the store. I haven't been here in ages, since we were little and my mom would drop me off to play with Nat while she shopped.

There's an old battered couch, and some file cabinets and a desk that looks like it's from a movie from the sixties, with an old desk lamp on it. On the wall is a framed announcement from an old issue of the local paper. The headline proclaims that Sammy is being named the president of the newly formed Brooklyn Heights and Cobble Hill Merchants Association.

Sammy points to the cabinets. "We used to keep all our records there. That was before computers. Now they're old and rusty. Like me."

Gus flops down on the couch and I join him. Sammy goes behind the desk and pulls out a chair on wheels with torn vinyl armrests. He eases into the chair carefully, making an "oomph" noise as his butt hits the seat. My dad has started making that noise when he sits down, I notice. I guess that's what happens as you get older.

Nat is standing warily by the door.

"Darling, close the door," he instructs her. "And join your friends."

Nat comes over and sits on the arm of the couch. It's

sagging already, and I think there is no way she's going to sit between us, all squeezed together.

"So tell me about this ghost," Sammy says, smiling.

I can't believe a grown-up is actually taking this seriously.

"It's not really a ghost, exactly," I begin. "More like a presence. I don't know. Weird things are happening."

"When did this start?"

"*Jidoo!* You're not telling me you actually believe in ghosts?" Nat practically screams.

"A little respect for your *jidoo,* Nat," Sammy says gently but firmly. "I've lived a few years more than you on this planet, so maybe you should listen instead of talk."

Nat crosses her arms. "You always brag about how good I am at school, how smart I am. Well, in science we learn to trust in what's real, what can be verified. Ghosts aren't real. Everybody knows that."

"Science doesn't know everything," Sammy says. "I was watching a show on TV last night—"

"On the History Channel, right?" Gus breaks in.

Sammy shoots him a look. "The History Channel? That's nothing but nonsense. No, this was on public television. With real scientists. I think it was called *Mysteries of Science.*"

"But—"

"Nat, darling, let me finish. We don't know a lot of things. Scientists don't even know why nine out of ten people are right-handed. Did you know that?"

"No," Nat says, "but that's different."

"And the bumblebee!" Gus says. "Scientists say the way it's designed it shouldn't fly, but it does!"

"That's different," Nat says. "Just because something can't be explained doesn't mean it's supernatural. There's an explanation for all the things that have been happening to Danny."

"You think they're all coincidences?" Sammy asks her. "Or that he's dreamed it up because he wanted the room for himself?"

"That's one answer," Nat says.

Sammy turns to me. "Well, Danny, what do *you* think?"

I'm quiet for a minute. We can hear all the noises of the bustling store outside: cash registers, numbers being called out, people chatting. In this normal, everyday world what I was feeling last night seems kind of silly. I look at Sammy's kindly face peering down at me and the words tumble out.

"All I know is that these things are happening. I mean, when I talk about it, it sounds stupid, and if any other kid was telling me about it, I'd think he was nuts. So . . . I just don't know."

Sammy reaches out and pats my arm with his huge calloused fingers. I look down and see a lifetime of stocking shelves, counting out change, and shaking his customers' hands.

Sammy looks straight into my eyes. It's a little unnerving. "Young man, I've lived in Brooklyn my entire seventy-nine years. I've worked at this store since I was younger than my granddaughter the genius here. And let me tell you, I've met all sorts of people and heard all sorts of stories. And after all of that, I have come to one conclusion."

He pauses.

"If I know anything, I know this—there are ghosts in Brooklyn."

CHAPTER 19

ALGEBRA AND COFFEE

A loud slapping noise breaks the silence. I don't know what it is at first, then realize it's Nat, face-palming. "*Jidoo,* how can you say that?"

Sammy turns to his granddaughter and emits another low, rumbling chuckle. "You know, sweetheart, I wouldn't say it if it wasn't true."

Gus swallows hard. "Have *you* ever seen one?"

Sammy smiles. "Me? Not really. Well, maybe I've known a few merchants who've disappeared with my money without delivering my order, but I'm not sure they count as ghosts."

Nat shakes her head. "You're only encouraging him."

Sammy brushes some crumbs off his pants. "I'm not exactly an expert on this. I know your *tayta* claims she's been visited by her late mother. You know what I say?"

"That you believe her?" I ask.

"No, I say if it *is* true, better her than me!" Sammy says, and laughs so hard at his own joke he starts to cough.

"There are no such thing as ghosts. They're just stories," insists Nat.

"Well, stories had to come from somewhere," I say.

Sammy nods in approval. "Good point! For example, did you know where ghouls come from?"

"Sure! From the cemetery!" says Gus loudly, the way he does in school when he completely misunderstands the question. I have to admire his confidence, but I wish he'd think a little harder.

Sam nods patiently. "Well, yes. But I mean originally."

"Let me guess," Nat says, like she's been here before. "It's an Arab word."

"Yes!" says Sammy proudly. "My little genius."

Nat reddens. "I'm not a genius. I just know when you ask that question the answer is always the Arab people, algebra, our numerals, coffee. . . ."

"Those were all from the Arabs?" Gus asks.

"Arab culture," Sammy gently corrects him. "And ghouls, while perhaps not as helpful as what Nat talks about, are from Arab traditions too."

Now Nat and I lean in, as if somehow the ghouls were listening.

"In Arab folklore, ghouls were demons who lived in

the desert who could take on any form," Sammy continues. "They especially like eating children, drinking their blood. They can even eat the dead, which is how we tend to think of them today."

Gus stares at me. "They eat children?"

"Only in the desert," Nat says, shaking her head. "In ancient times, when children wandered off, hyenas probably ate them. And people came up with folktales to scare kids into staying with their families."

Sammy nods. "You're probably right." He winks at Gus and me. "Nat, there was another story about a ghoul you loved me to tell when you were little. Remember?"

There is a look in Nat's eyes as she softens. "From *A Thousand and One Nights,* right?"

"'The Story of Sidi-Nouman'!" she and Sammy say in unison.

Sammy turns to us. "Perhaps you'd like to hear it?"

Gus and I nod and settle into the old couch.

CHAPTER 20

THE STORY OF SIDI-NOUMAN

Sidi-Nouman was a young man of good birth and modest fortune. As is tradition among his people, he did not set eyes upon his wife-to-be until their wedding day. So he was enchanted to discover that she was beautiful in every way, and he looked forward to a long, happy married life.

But from their first meal together, Sidi-Nouman discovered something strange. Instead of eating her rice with a spoon like most people, his wife took a pin out of a small case she carried and ate only a few grains. The same with the other courses, from breads to meat.

Sidi-Nouman tried to convince her that they had money to spare, and she could eat her fill. But she continued to eat in this strange manner, not even enough to fill a sparrow.

This went on for days, with his new wife never answering him about her strange behavior.

Finally, one night, as Sidi-Nouman lay in bed, he felt his wife get up and dress herself and slip out of the house. He determined to follow her, and in the moonlight he saw her meet up with a female ghoul. He watched in horror as his wife and her hideous companion made their way to the cemetery, where they dug up a corpse that had been buried that very day and feasted on her flesh, cheerfully chatting all the while. When they had finished, they threw the remains back in the grave and replaced the dirt, which they had disturbed so terribly.

In great distress, Sidi-Nouman returned to his home, a plan forming in his head. His wife, her appetite for human flesh sated, returned to join him, none the wiser.

The next night, his ghoulish bride was picking at her food as usual, when he said to her, "Amina, my love, I offer you the choicest of foods, none of which you seem to enjoy. Is it possible that there is none among them that tastes as sweet as the flesh of a corpse?"

No sooner had Sidi-Nouman uttered these words than Amina, seized with fury upon being discovered, grabbed a vessel of water, and plunging her hand in it, murmured some words under her breath. Then, sprinkling the water on his face, she cried madly: "Wretch, receive the reward of your prying, and become a dog."

As soon as the words left her mouth, poor Sidi-Nouman

found himself transformed into a dog, which his wretched wife began to beat with a stick. Happily for him, he was able to escape from the house, with only a sore tail to show for it.

Howling in pain, the poor animal wandered the streets, attacked by other dogs and kicked by merchants and travelers alike. Finally, a kindly baker took pity on the wounded creature, giving him shelter and a few crusts of bread to eat. The baker called him Rufus, and greatly enjoyed the company of his new friend and companion.

One day, a woman came in to buy bread, and one of the coins she paid with was a false one. She refused to admit it, and as a joke, the baker said, "It is such a bad imitation that even my dog would not be taken in. Here, Rufus! Rufus!"

Rufus jumped onto the counter. The baker threw down the woman's money before him and said, "Find out if there is a bad coin." Rufus laid his paw on the false one, surprising both the baker and his customer, who produced another coin in its place.

Of course news of such a dog spread throughout the village, and soon all were bringing their coins to see if Rufus could spot the fake one, which he could at every try.

This went on for some time, until one day a woman who had never been in the store put six coins on the counter and Rufus, as always, found the false coin. She gazed at him for some time, and then left the shop making a sign for him to follow her secretly.

Rufus waited until the baker was occupied at his oven and slipped out the door. He found the woman, who took him to her home, where a beautiful girl was working at a piece of embroidery. "My daughter!" exclaimed the woman. "I have brought you the famous dog belonging to the baker that can tell good money from bad. You know that when I first heard of him, I told you I was sure he must be a man, changed into a dog by magic."

"You are right, Mother," replied the girl, who got up and dipped her hand into a vessel of water. Sprinkling it over Rufus, she said, "If you were born dog, remain dog; but if you were born man, by virtue of this water resume your proper form."

In one moment the spell was broken. The dog's shape vanished as if it had never been, and it was a man who stood before the woman and her daughter.

Sidi-Nouman told them his whole story, and finished by begging the mother to let him return the favor.

"Sidi-Nouman," said the daughter, "say no more about the obligation you are under to us. The knowledge that we have been of service to you is ample payment. Let us speak of Amina, your wife, with whom I was acquainted before her marriage. She and I studied magic under the same mistress. Please do not concern yourself with repaying us. But it is not enough to have broken your spell—Amina must be punished for her wickedness. Remain for a moment with my mother, I beg you," she added. "I will return shortly."

The daughter soon came back with a small bottle in her hand.

She told Sidi-Nouman, "Go home, then, without delay, and await Amina's return in your room. When she enters the house, go to meet her. In her surprise, she will try to run away. Have this bottle ready, and dash the water it contains over her, saying boldly, 'Receive the reward of your crimes.' That is all I have to tell you."

Sidi-Nouman did as the girl told him, and he had not been in my house many minutes before Amina returned. As she approached the bedroom, he stepped in front of her, with the water in his hand.

Amina gave one loud cry and turned to the door, but she was too late—Sidi-Nouman had already dashed the water in her face and spoken the magic words. Amina disappeared, and in her place stood a horse! Sidi-Nouman ordered the horse to be taken to his stables. From that day forward, he rode the horse, and treated her well, although she had been so terrible to him.

As Sammy finishes the story, he leans back in his chair and takes a swig of water.

I look over at Nat, who is sitting with her legs pulled up, hugging them to her chest.

Gus rubs his eyes. "That was one heck of a bedtime story! I wouldn't sleep for a week if my grandpa told me that!"

Sammy shrugs. "It has a happy ending. And a nice dog."

"And it's a fairy tale!" Nat says. "That stuff is all made up."

Sammy nods. "True, my little scientist. Still, I keep waiting for a nice golden retriever to show up and help me count out my change!"

I swallow hard, with Sammy's great gray eyes peering down at me under his bushy eyebrows.

Then he bursts into laughter. "But don't listen to me! My granddaughter is the smart one in the family."

Before Nat can answer, there is a knock on the door. Luuk peers in.

"There you are!" he says, beaming. "We've been looking for you! We were afraid you were spirited away by ghosts!"

Sammy rises and ushers us out into the bustling store. "Please excuse my keeping them from you. I was just—"

"Telling us some old corny jokes," Nat says, shutting down the conversation.

We head to the door.

"So what brings you to Brooklyn, if you don't mind?" Sammy asks. As soon as he hears that Luuk teaches at Utrecht University he looks excited. "Are you aware that the Dutch were the first settlers from Europe in Brooklyn?"

"After the Native Americans," Nat says.

"Darling, I said *from Europe,*" her grandfather says evenly.

Daan looks up from the bag of nuts he has been devouring. "Of course. We were here first. By rights this should still be New Amsterdam."

"And did you know there was a New Utrecht here?" Sammy asks triumphantly, "And even now there is a New Utrecht High School, which has been there for more than one hundred years."

Luuk looks delighted. "Where is it? Perhaps I could visit!"

Daan checks his watch. "I don't think we have time. Your lecture is in five hours and we have to get back to the apartment and shower and change, and you need to rehearse."

Luuk rolls his eyes. "Yes, Mama."

It's weird hearing them talk about going back to "the apartment" and realizing that they mean the place where I live. The other thing I realize is that after staying here just one day, Luuk and Daan are starting to feel like friends.

Nat and Gus walk us back to "the apartment." After Daan and Luuk go in, I linger with Nat and Gus on the stoop, sharing some chocolate-covered cashews (we never leave Haddad's empty-handed). Fun fact: before going in, Luuk told us that "stoop" is actually from the Dutch word for "steps." It goes back to Amsterdam, where steps protected the houses from floods, since so much of the city is on low-lying land.

"Your grandfather sure knows a lot about Brooklyn," Gus says casually.

Nat perches on the railing. "And he sure loves to talk about it."

We sit there, thinking of everything Sammy has said.

"So . . . ," Gus begins. "What if there's another knock on your door tonight?"

Nat jumps off the railing and pushes him. "You're really not helping things." She turns to me. "Danny, please tell me you understand these are all probably just coincidences and things in your head, right?"

"Maybe," I say. "But isn't it a little weird that the memory card failed, and my mom wasn't able to—"

Nat holds up her hands. "Stop. This is what happens. Memory cards fail all the time. It happened at my nephew's christening. And your mom's laptop crashes all the time. You're always complaining about it."

She has a point. "Okay, what about the other stuff?" I ask.

"We put things together because they fit what we want to think. You wouldn't think twice about these things if you hadn't been thinking about ghosts and stuff. Stop it, Gus, that's disgusting."

Gus is picking a piece of cashew out of his teeth. "So you think Danny just imagined the other stuff, like the knocking?"

Nat looks at me.

"I'm not nuts," I say. "It felt really real. I swear I wasn't dreaming."

"Yeah, well . . . just don't freak out. Tell yourself this isn't real. This isn't happening. Or that there's a logical explanation. Because there is."

I look out onto the street. The early-autumn Brooklyn sunshine dapples the leaves on the trees. "Everything you say sounds great now. I just hope I feel the same way tonight."

Gus laughs. "Yeah, good luck with that, buddy."

CHAPTER 21

LITTLE SQUIRREL BREAD

I am still up when Luuk and Daan quietly turn the key in the lock. Mom and Dad went to bed and left them a note, along with a bottle of wine for them to celebrate with.

I hear them shushing each other as they take off their jackets and ties. I wander into the kitchen.

"You're still up!" Luuk says pleasantly as he takes something wrapped in foil out of his bag. He indicates it. "Some very good cheese left over from the reception, and crackers. We thought your mama and papa would enjoy them."

These are two of the most thoughtful people I've ever met.

There is a small sighing noise as Daan eases the cork from the bottle of wine. "A California cabernet! How did your parents know we love cabernet?"

"I think you mentioned it this morning at breakfast," I say. "My mom bought some for her and my dad as well."

Daan takes out three glasses. He pours some in two and turns to me. "Will you join us?"

"I'm not allowed to drink," I say, kind of shocked. "I'm only thirteen."

"Please forgive Daan," Luuk says. "We are used to Europe. Babies drink over there."

I laugh.

"He's serious!" Daan says. "You put a little on your finger and give it to them when they're teething! And then, when you're older, Mama or Papa lets you finish their glass."

Luuk takes a sip. "It's really very good. I need to remember to tell your parents." He looks at me. "So what is keeping you up so late? Playing video games, I expect?"

"Actually, I wanted to hear how your speech went," I lie. The truth is that I just couldn't fall asleep. I kept thinking about Sammy's stories about flesh-eating ghouls, and everything that's happened since we decided to rent out the bedroom.

Luuk shrugs. "It went okay. Some people seemed to like it."

Daan gives Luuk a big hug. "He is being modest. It was a huge success. Everyone told me it was the most brilliant presentation of the whole conference."

Luuk says something to Daan in Dutch. Either that or he's clearing his throat. It's hard to tell sometimes.

Daan looks over at me. "I was not exaggerating, Danny. You know I tell the truth. We Daans have to stick together, right?"

"Right," I say, grinning. They really are like two big kids sometimes.

Luuk yawns. "Well, we have an early flight tomorrow. It's too bad our visit is so short. Maybe next time we stay a few more days, yes?"

"You're coming back?" I ask.

"I would come back just to go to that amazing store!" Daan says.

They head to their room after making sure I'm done in the bathroom. Thoughtful as ever.

I suddenly feel very tired. Like having the two of them in the house protects it, somehow. Even though last night there was that knocking. I'm pretty sure I can make it through tonight without any more weird dreams.

I pass out as soon as I hit my bed, and sleep better than I have in days. I don't remember any dreams, and if someone *had* knocked on my door, I was so out I didn't hear it. The next thing I know, I'm smelling bacon and seeing light under my door.

It's funny, having spent almost every night of my life sleeping in here. Whenever we go anywhere (like when we visit relatives), it's hard for me to sleep in a room with a window. I'm just not used to it.

I stretch, get out of bed, and open the door to see my parents and Luuk and Daan already at the table.

"Good morning, sleepyhead!" my mom calls out.

"How do you say 'sleepyhead' in Dutch?" my dad asks Luuk.

"Same thing, pretty much," he says. "We say *slaapkop.*"

I join them and take a plate. "It sounds funnier in Dutch."

"Everything sounds funnier in Dutch!" says Daan. "You know those mushrooms that you put in pasta—what are they in English again?"

Luuk has clearly heard this before. "Porcini."

Daan nods. "You know them, yes?"

"Of course," my mom says. "We love them."

"We call them *eekhoorntjesbrood,* which literally means 'little squirrel's bread'!"

While I think this is cute, my parents think it is the funniest thing in the world.

My dad wants to write it down. "I bet even Sammy doesn't know that!"

"I wouldn't count on it," Luuk says. "That man knows more about food than anyone I've ever met."

There is a buzzing noise and Daan checks his phone. "Ach! That is a text telling me our car will be here in two minutes! We really need to get going!"

He jumps up and heads to the door. I see that their suit-cases are already packed and ready to go.

Luuk sighs and bows to my mother. "Maureen, thank you again for such a lovely visit."

"Did you like the wine?" she asks anxiously. "I don't know much about it. I asked at the store."

"It was superb," Daan says, helping Luuk with his coat.

As they rush to leave, promises are made that if we are ever in Holland we must let them know, and of course they will keep in touch.

The door closes and there is quiet.

It's odd. I thought that having guests would be the worst thing possible.

"I'm going to miss them," I say.

My dad nods. "I know. It's funny, isn't it?"

My mom is rinsing the dishes. "I'm afraid they've spoiled us. I have a feeling not all our guests are going to be so nice."

CHAPTER 22

THE CRUCIBLE OF ARMPIT SMELLS

That night at dinner my mom laughs to herself. My dad asks what's up.

"Oh, it's nothing," my mom says. "I was just remembering something Daan said. . . ."

This sets off a recitation of all the clever things our house-guests said, how thoughtful they were, and how sophisticated.

Oh, swell.

Now that Jake is gone and we have the whole AirHotel thing squared away, we'll spend every dinner talking about somebody *else*.

I wipe my mouth with my napkin. "I have homework to do. Is it okay if I go to my room?"

"Sure, sweetheart," my mom says. "Just don't stay up too

late. Daan told me you were up when they came home last night."

"You really need to get your sleep," my dad adds. "Especially on a weekday."

I want to tell them that it's hard to sleep when there's something going on in this apartment that's totally creeping me out, but I know they'll just say I've got to get used to the new situation.

I put in my earbuds, crank up some music on my phone, and lose myself in taking notes for a paper I need to write for English. It's about this play called *The Crucible* that Mrs. Yuli has been reading out loud.

A crucible, in case you don't know (I didn't, though Nat did), is a container used in science to combine things at a high temperature.

But this play isn't about science. It's about a town where all the elements are combined to create something that burns through the people who live there. That's actually pretty good. I write that down as my topic sentence.

It's kind of based on the Salem witch trials, where these girls accused another girl of being a witch and the whole town believed them. Later, the narrator explains that it's similar to the time the playwright Arthur something (wait, I need to know that for my paper—oh, right, Arthur Miller) was accused of being a Communist in the fifties, and he was writing about how people can be gripped by hysteria and manipulated into believing something that isn't true. I'm not really explaining the plot all that well. There's more to it, but this is the part I keep coming back to.

The girls in the play aren't really witches, but they convince people that some of them are by making up stuff.

Is that what my parents think is going on?

Is that what Nat thinks?

That I'm just making this up?

All this thinking is making me tired. Mom is right. I need a good night's sleep.

"Just leave me alone tonight, okay?" I hear myself saying out loud.

My dad calls to me, faintly, from outside my room. "Did you say something?"

The door opens and he's standing there.

"Uh, no," I say, pulling off my earbuds, "I was just . . . singing along with some music. I guess I didn't realize how loud I was."

He makes a face. "How many times have we told you to keep the volume down on those things? You don't want to be deaf like Nana Helene, do you?"

Nana Helene is my dad's mother. She nods and smiles at everything you say, then pats you on the wrist and you realize she hasn't heard a word you've said.

"It's down, it's *down*," I insist.

My dad shakes his head. "Yikes."

My mom appears at the door with a towel. "Time for a shower and then bed, young man."

She actually said that without adding how Jake used to take a shower every night and go to bed without being told. I have to admit I'm stunned.

The bathroom looks so empty without all of Daan's and Luuk's various creams and lotions. I mean, we *had* shampoo and conditioner and stuff for them, but I guess they didn't use ours.

"Should I use the unopened shampoo and conditioner?" I yell.

"No!" my mom screams. (I told you she screams about everything.) "Save those for the next guests!"

She opens the door a crack and hands me the shampoo and stuff from their bathroom.

Oh, yuck. Now I'm going to smell like them?

"And use deodorant!" she yells from the other side of the door. "You stink!"

This is a new thing. I never used to stink.

I realize that now my armpit is a crucible. I like this word.

So I take my shower, and keep thinking about those horror movies where a murderer comes in and stabs you in the shower, which makes it like the shortest shower ever.

I pad down the hallway back to my tiny room.

I settle into bed hoping for no scary dreams or anything weird. I hear the murmur of my parents talking in the other room. There is some laughter, and I can picture them at their respective workstations.

When I tell my friends that my parents work in the same room all day, most of them think it's weird. They have parents who go off to jobs in offices and spend the day with other people. I'd rather be like my parents. They are like best friends who are married.

Anyhow, I just love the sound of them in the front room talking low like this. It makes me feel so safe and protected, and it soothes me to sleep.

When I wake up in the middle of the night to use the bathroom, it's quiet, except the usual street noises: the occasional car passing by downstairs, sirens in the distance.

I yawn and get up and open my door.

The light in Jake's room is on. Someone is in there.

CHAPTER 23

FACETIME

Not again. Maybe it's my dad. Sometimes he has trouble sleeping and will read for a while. He'll usually do it in the front room, though.

My parents' room is across the hall from mine, so I tiptoe over. They leave their door open (unless we have company), so I peer in and see that they are both there. My dad is snoring softly.

Now what? Another dream?

I try my best to take deep breaths.

There has to be a simple explanation. My mom could have been cleaning in there after I went to sleep, and left the light on.

Like my mother would ever leave a light on when she left a room.

But it's possible.

I want more than anything to just go into my room and close the door and pretend I saw nothing. Then in the morning my mom can yell at my dad for leaving the light on when he was in there earlier, and I'll be fine.

But something is pushing me down the hallway. This is not a dream. I know it's not. It's just a room. With a light on.

Right?

I reach for the doorknob and try to swallow, but I can't because my mouth is so dry.

I try to turn the knob, but my hands are shaking and so damp they keep slipping. Finally I grab the doorknob and yank the door open.

Is that someone by the window?

A girl is staring back at me.

I want to run but force myself to look again.

Stupid me, it's just my reflection.

I take a deep breath to calm myself down. And then another.

Just look around the room, Danny. . . .

See? It's empty. Nothing to be afraid of.

I reach for the light switch to turn off the light. I see my arm and hand are shiny.

That's when I realize I'm drenched in sweat.

I am *so glad* I used that deodorant. But I can smell the fear.

There's nothing here. Nothing. I mean, not like in the movies.

No voices, no blood coming out of the walls.

Just the same bland Ikea furniture.

But there *is* something. I swear, I can feel it. Like someone is watching me. I can't get out of here fast enough.

I leave the room before reaching back and switching off the light. As quickly as I can, I shut the door behind me.

I close my eyes and use my T-shirt to wipe the sweat dripping from my forehead.

In the bathroom, I feel my heartbeat getting slower, and I turn on the sink and put my arms under the tap. The cool water is the perfect antidote to whatever I was feeling before. It's real, and as I splash the water onto my face I can feel the fear washing off. I can just hear Nat's voice: *ridiculous.*

I leave the bathroom and head for my room.

Then, out of the corner of my eye, I catch sight of something behind me.

Under Jake's door, there is a glowing light.

"It seems to be working fine." Gabriel is switching the light on and off.

It's morning.

There was no way I was going back into Jake's room last night. I know, what a shocker, right?

I just ran to my room and shut the door and climbed back into bed. Not that I slept all that much.

Of course, in the morning, the light in Jake's room is off. And both my parents swear they didn't go in there to turn it off. So my dad calls Gabriel to have him check the switch.

"Sometimes in humid weather things like this happen," Gabriel explains. "But I'll change the switch and see if that makes a difference." My dad nods like he understands. My dad wants Gabriel to think he is a guy who understands how things like light switches and electricity work.

I want to believe Gabriel, although nothing like this has ever happened before in all the years we've lived here.

As Gabriel lets himself out, there's an alert from Mom's laptop and she excitedly calls us over to the table. This is our first FaceTime call with Jake since he's gone to school.

After a brief pause, Jake is there, looking a little bleary and unshaven.

"Jaaake!" our parents scream together.

He winces, then laughs. "Not so loud, okay? My roommates are still sleeping."

"It's noon!" Dad says, also laughing. "Out partying last night?"

Jake rubs his eyes and then opens them wide, like he's just gotten up himself. "Yeah, not really a party. Just kind of a get-together."

"That sounds nice!" our mom says in a voice so chirpy it's almost as creepy as last night.

"Mom, chill out," Jake says. "You're talking weird."

Mom's face crumples. "I'm sorry. I was just trying to, you know, take an interest."

"We're a little hyped about seeing you, is all," our dad adds, sounding ridiculously amped.

"I know, I'm happy to see you too, but I can hear you fine if you speak normal," Jake says. He looks past them and waves at me. "Hey, bro!"

I wave back. "Yo."

This is a universal big brother–little brother greeting. We are definitely not going to make a big deal about this.

Our parents ask him about his classes, whether he's eating enough, if he's made any friends. The way our mom says "friends" makes Jake crack up.

"No, Mom, I haven't made any 'friends,'" Jake says, putting the word in air quotes.

"I wasn't asking about girls," our mom says, and sniffs.

"Riiight." Jake catches my eye, and I laugh with him. All of a sudden his face changes expression.

"Who is that with you guys?"

I turn around, but there's no one there. "What are you talking about?"

"Stop messing with me. There's a girl. Right behind you."

CHAPTER 24

THE PHANTOM GIGGLER

There's definitely no one there. I feel a huge sense of relief. I am not crazy. My brother saw her too.

Dad turns around. "Oh, that's Jenny Schwartz. I'm doing her bat mitzvah video." He's looking at the monitor on his desk. Indeed, there is a close-up of a blond girl with braces on my dad's screen.

Jake looks skeptical. He peers into his phone. "Yeah . . . I guess that was it. I can't really see it now, but it looked a lot bigger before. Like she was right over Danny's shoulder."

"I think it's where my laptop is," our mom explains. "It makes things look closer than they are."

"Like your new girlfriend over *your* shoulder," I say.

Jake jumps like someone stuck a hot poker up his butt. He whirls around, looking off camera.

"Psych!" I shout. I don't usually get him like that. "But now we know you have a new girlfriend!"

Even over FaceTime we can see Jake turning all sorts of colors. "Shut up, Danny. I just thought someone had snuck into the room."

"So . . . anything you want to tell us?" Mom asks.

Just in case you're wondering, I'm enjoying this so much.

"No! I mean, she's not my girlfriend!" Jake blurts out.

Dad nods. "Uh, okay. So *who* is not your girlfriend?"

Jake looks offscreen. In the background we hear a giggle.

"So who's that?" Mom sure is persistent.

"My roommate!" Jake says quickly.

"Your roommate giggles like a girl," I say.

There's a cascade of giggles, which seems to make Jake even more anxious.

"He giggles like a girl, okay? He's very self-conscious about it."

He hits someone, and the giggling is muffled.

"Look, I gotta go study," he says quickly. "Love you guys! Call you next week!"

Before our parents can answer, he clicks off his phone.

There is general hysteria in the Kantrowitz household, and with all the talk of this mystery girl, I almost forget about everything that's been going on.

It feels like old times, teasing Jake about girls and seeing him get all flustered about it. Every time he went on a date in high school he would do everything he could to not tell our parents, because, let's face it, they would ask the girl something dumb, or act all weird around her, like fake parents.

Last summer Jake met a girl named Annie when he went to work at a summer camp in Maine. He made the mistake of posting pictures of the two of them on Facebook. Our mother somehow did *not* think it weird or wrong to post comments about what a lovely couple they were, and how she looked forward to meeting Annie sometime.

You can imagine that didn't go over too well with Jake. Especially since Annie ended up cheating on him with the swimming instructor, who was some dirtbag freshman from Williams College who was named, for real, Chad. I asked Jake if Chad popped the collar on his polo shirt, and Jake said, "You know it, bro," and then actually laughed, for real, at something *I'd* said.

This was one of the greatest moments of our brotherhood.

"Well," my mom says, "if he won't tell us who she is, I guess I'll just call her the Phantom Giggler!"

"She strikes in the dead of the morning," my dad riffs. "Maybe Jake's room at college is haunted too!" Because of course he doesn't know when to stop.

"That's *not* funny," I say.

Mom rubs the top of my head. "Honey, I know the apartment feels weird since Jake left, and you don't like changes—"

"Mom, what are you talking about?"

"Danny, you broke out in a rash when you moved from kindergarten to first grade, remember?"

I cannot believe this. "No, I do not remember. That was like a hundred years ago. And what does that have to do with the fact that I seem to be the only one in this apartment who *is being haunted*?" I practically yell.

"It's just that you've never dealt well with change . . . ," my dad says gently.

"So you both think I'm just imagining all this?" I ask, walking away from them.

"Danny . . . ," he starts.

"You just think all this stuff is a coincidence?"

Mom stands next to him. Uh-oh. A united front. "Our minds put things together sometimes and create narratives."

"*Sammy* says there are ghosts in Brooklyn," I insist.

"I think he was speaking about Brooklyn in kind of poetic terms," Mom says. "You know, because this part of Brooklyn has such a rich and long history. It's easy to imagine all the people who've lived here before us."

"He was *not* talking about that," I answer. "Sammy is a lot of things, but he isn't a poet. He meant real ghosts. Ask Nat."

My dad takes a swig from his mug. "Sammy's quite the storyteller."

I look from one of them to the other. "So you really refuse to even consider it?"

My mom sighs. "It's easier to imagine this stuff when you're thirteen, Danny."

There is a crashing noise from Jake's room.

We freeze.

"Did I imagine that?" I demand, and we rush down the hallway to Jake's room.

We reach the doorway and peer in.

The framed Ikea print has fallen off the wall and is lying on the floor, a jumble of broken wood and bits of glass.

My mom turns. "I'll get the broom."

I face my dad. He's rubbing the back of his neck.

"I . . . guess . . . the picture hook couldn't bear that much weight." He sighs. "One more thing for Gabriel to take care of before our next guest."

My mom has returned and is sweeping up the debris on the floor. "It's a good thing that didn't happen when anyone was staying here."

My dad is putting on his coat. "I'll get a new frame at the shop on Atlantic Avenue." He catches my mom's look. "It's a standard size. They're premade. It won't be expensive." He turns to me. "You want to come?"

I run to join him. Anything to get out of this apartment.

CHAPTER 25

THE GHOST BOYFRIEND

"You live in an old apartment," Nat says, peering at the candy arrayed in front of her. "Light switches break. Old walls don't always hold picture hooks."

"And girls' faces just pop up behind you," Gus adds, making his selection.

It's Monday after school, and we're at Harry's.

Harry's is a little grocery store tucked into the bottom of an apartment building. I think it's always been there—it was here when my dad was a kid, but back then it was owned by a Greek family. Now it's owned by a Korean family.

That's the way it is in Brooklyn. Around the corner there's a barbershop run by a Russian guy named Serge who's been cutting everybody's hair for as long as I can remember. Next door to him is a dry cleaners that's owned by an Indian family.

And a block away is a stationery store where everyone working there is Orthodox Jewish and talks to each other in Yiddish. I swear you can walk three blocks and hear like eight languages spoken. And that's not counting all the tourists!

By the way, Harry isn't the name of the owner of the store. Nobody knows who Harry was. The guy behind the counter is Joe, the son of the guy who owns it. You've never met a more cheerful person in your life. He isn't that much older than Jake, maybe in his twenties. But he's always nice to us kids, and learns each of our names. He's kind of amazing that way.

It's one of those weird warm days in autumn where you start out wearing a coat, and by lunch you're wearing a sweater and then by the time school's over it's gotten so you're down to your T-shirt.

We stopped in at Harry's on our way to Brooklyn Bridge Park to play some Frisbee. They've got all sorts of candy that costs as little as a nickel, so even if you have only fifty cents or a dollar you can get a lot.

Joe greets us. "Hey, Nat! Hi, Gus! What's up, Danny?"

"Danny's apartment is haunted," Gus tells Joe as he picks out his candy.

Joe laughs. "That's crazy!"

"Thank you," Nat says. "I've been telling them that for weeks."

Joe tallies up what we owe while Gus takes it upon himself

to relate all the weird things that have been going on. He only exaggerates a little.

"There wasn't any moaning," I object. "And I guess there might be another explanation."

"Hey!" An old lady prods me with her cane. Clearly we're taking too much time.

"Two quick picks and a five-box across, right, Margie?" Joe says, pulling the scratch-off tickets from a strip hanging from a rack behind him. He always knows everyone's order.

She nods and carefully takes her money out of an old beat-up wallet. As she opens the wallet I see an old faded photo of a young girl in a plastic card holder. I wonder if it's her daughter. Or maybe a granddaughter. It's funny to think of this crabby old lady as a mom.

"What're you looking at?" she snaps at me.

"Nothing," I say, backing away.

"Nosy kids," she mutters, and heads off to see if she's won anything.

Joe turns back to us. "Or maybe you have a *gwishin*."

"A what?" asks Gus.

"In Korea, we have *gwishin*. They're like spirits of dead people who have unfinished business here on earth, and are cursed to haunt the place they died until they can complete whatever they need to do before moving on to the afterlife," Joe explains.

Nat closes her eyes. "You don't really believe that, do you, Joe?"

Joe laughs. "Nah, but they make movies about them all the time. Especially *cheonyeo gwishin*. Those are girls who die before they can be married. Sometimes they haunt a house and torment the family until they find them a suitable ghost boyfriend."

"You're making that up," Gus says.

"Nope, ask my grandma. She says they had one in her village when she was a little girl. At least, they all believed they did."

"Where would you find a ghost boyfriend anyway?" I ask.

"Maybe there's an online ghost dating service," Gus says, unwrapping a piece of bubble gum.

"That's the dumbest thing I've ever heard," Nat snaps.

Gus nods. "You're right. I mean, they couldn't even use an app, right? You can't swipe right if you don't have hands."

Joe looks like he's trying hard not to laugh. "Good point, Gus."

Nat grabs a few pieces of candy and throws a quarter on the counter. "And anyway, this isn't a Korean village, it's Brooklyn Heights."

Joe nods. "True that, Nat. I was just kidding with Danny. I don't think you have a *gwishin*. From what I know, they're not very shy about showing themselves."

There's a commotion at the door. A bunch of kids from one of the other schools in the neighborhood are coming in—they're our age, but with way nicer shoes and backpacks. Joe greets them all by name of course, and they wave and go toward the back where the full-size candy bars and drinks are. A girl turns to her friend and asks if she can borrow five dollars.

As she turns back I see her sweatshirt says SAINT ANSELM in big letters.

I've got nothing against private school kids—I mean, it's not their fault their parents have money to send them to "good schools"—but sometimes I am a little jealous. I bet they all have nice big bedrooms.

With windows.

Not one renovated closet dweller among them, I'm pretty sure.

As more kids pile into the narrow shop, this time older ones from the high school who are louder and more obnoxious, we wave goodbye to Joe and head to the park.

"Did you see the sneakers on that kid with the curly blond hair?" Nat asks. "I saw those online. They cost like two hundred bucks."

Gus reaches up and grabs a red leaf off one of the trees lining the block. They're turning color already.

"He probably has a whole closet of them," I say.

"You don't know that," Nat says. But she looks kind of sad.

"We could go back and ask," Gus suggests.

We all crack up.

It feels so normal. Everything is the same.

Joe's the same. The private school kids are the same.

Our jokes are the same.

But I know when I go back home, it's not going to feel the same. Something has changed there since Jake left. Maybe it's just me. Maybe I'm just making this stuff up in my head.

But what if I'm not?

CHAPTER 26

MRS. SARAH DELANO CABOT AND HER DAUGHTER ALICE

I open the door to our apartment and my nose is immediately assailed by the smell of bleach.

My heart sinks. If Mom is cleaning, it means we're going to have another visitor. I knew there was someone scheduled, but it kind of snuck up on me.

"Sarah Delano Cabot and her daughter Alice," my mom says breathlessly at dinner the night before they're scheduled to arrive.

"Sarah Delano Cabot," my father drawls, in his best approximation of a prep school student. "*Delighted* to meet you. Care for a gin and tonic? Where's your husband, Chip? Oh, his actual name is Porter Delano Cabot the Third? I *do* apologize. How unforgivably *rude* of me."

This is pretty much how my dad acts whenever anyone with what he considers an overly old-fashioned name is mentioned.

My mom reddens and then goes back to her salad. "Get it out of your system now."

"I'll be a good boy," my father promises. "I just cannot for the life of me figure out why someone with a name like that would want to stay here instead of a nice hotel."

"Don't you remember Emily Stanton?" my mom asks. "The one who worked with me at the settlement house? She wore cardigans a lot."

"Did I meet her?" Dad asks.

My mom makes a "don't be an idiot of course you met her" noise and turns to me. "You did too. Remember the girl in the cardigan who came here to work on some cases when the pipes burst at the office? Like two years ago?"

"I don't think so," I say. "Wait. Now I remember. Was she the one . . . in the . . . *cardigan*?"

My dad stifles a laugh as my mom throws her napkin at me. "You two think you're so funny."

"Okay, okay," my dad says, surrendering. "So what about her?"

"I used to talk about her all the time," my mom says. "She came from one of the oldest families in Brooklyn. They can trace their lineage back to the Revolution. There was so much money there."

"Yes, and—" my dad says, making his "there is much too much detail in this story get to the point already" noise.

"The point is," my mom says acidly, "that she was so funny about money. I guess you would say she was 'thrifty.'"

"Wait, I *do* remember," I say. "Wasn't she the one who reused tea bags?"

My mom's eyes brighten with victory. *"Exactly.* And she never wore makeup, and she always wore a cardigan that was so mended it must have belonged to her mother. Maybe Mrs. Cabot is like that. They don't like to spend money."

My dad studies the printout my mom has handed him. "What are the Delano Cabots doing in New York?"

"I'm not sure," my mom says. "It was a last-minute booking."

"So how old is this Alice?" I ask.

I can just see a little kid running around here. The last thing I need. And then she'll become possessed and start throwing up pea soup like in that old move about an exorcism that's on the classic movie channel every Halloween that Dad told me about but still doesn't let me watch.

My dad checks the paper and his eyebrows raise. "Seventeen? Do they know they're sharing a bed?"

My mom shrugs. "Of course. I made a point of telling them."

My dad reads their address. "They're from Deer Isle,

Maine. Maybe they're used to it. Maybe up there it gets so cold you have to bunk together."

"Please don't ask them," my mom begs.

"Oh, I promise," my dad says, none too convincingly.

The Cabots are supposed to arrive in the morning, and that night, I wait for something to happen. Anything. Flashing lights, moans, noises in the dark.

Nothing.

It's like the room is holding its breath.

Like it knows someone new is coming.

Promptly at check-in (three o'clock) the doorbell rings, and we are graced with the formidable presence of Mrs. Sarah Delano Cabot.

Her gray hair is parted in the middle and falls straight down to her shoulders, where it kind of curls at the ends. It's like she hasn't changed her hairstyle since college or something. Behind simple steel eyeglasses, she has what I hear my mom later describe to my dad under her breath as "China blue" eyes, and she's wearing a windbreaker over a faded purple sweater.

"Come in, come in!" my mom trills as she greets them.

Mrs. Cabot reads from the paper in her hand. "You are Mrs. Kantrowitz?"

"Yes," my mother says. "But please call me Maureen."

My dad reaches out to shake her hand. "And I'm Marty."

Mrs. Cabot regards his hand for a moment before briskly shaking it. "I am Mrs. Sarah Delano Cabot. My daughter Alice is fetching our bags from the taxi."

My mom compliments Mrs. Sarah Delano Cabot (it will become an inside joke in my family to always refer to her with all three names) on her sweater.

"Did you order it from Bays' End?" my mom asks.

Mrs. Sarah Delano Cabot arches an eyebrow. I'm not kidding. Like for real. Like a character in a movie. And when she speaks she has a deep raspy voice. The words kind of drip out.

"A *catalog*?" She says it like it's the most exotic thing in the world. "Why, no. I knit."

Her daughter has brought up their luggage.

Unlike her mother, Alice has her hair in a long loose braid, and has an open, oval face. She has a DEER ISLE LACROSSE jacket on.

I notice that unlike Daan and Luuk, their suitcases are scuffed and appear to be handed down from generations, Cabot to Cabot. Or maybe Delano to Delano.

"Mother knits because there's nothing else to do up in Maine," she says.

Mrs. Sarah Delano Cabot turns to her daughter and laughs. Okay, not a real laugh. One of those "ha ha you and I are going to have a talk later" laughs. I'm beginning to think that she's scarier than the apartment ghost.

"I gave the man five dollars, Mother," Alice adds, before introducing herself to us.

"Whatever for, dear?" Mrs. Sarah Delano Cabot asks, jaw clenched. It's hard to tell if it's actually clenched more, because it's kind of been clenched since she got here.

Alice rolls her eyes. "Mother, you didn't tip him. He drove us all the way from Penn Station."

"He was very rude," Mrs. Sarah Delano Cabot says, "and hard to understand."

Alice gives me a look that says "this is what I deal with." "You know, Mother, he can't help the fact that he was born in another country."

Another dry-as-dust laugh from Mrs. Sarah Delano Cabot. "I remember coming to New York when I was your age. The cabbies were all American then. How times have changed."

Alice bites her lip. It's clear she wants to leave the room before her mom says anything else.

"I'll show you to the bedroom," I say, grabbing their bags.

"My hero," Alice says, and follows me.

I decide I like Alice.

I don't mean in that way. Just that she's a cool person.

CHAPTER 27

NIGHTY NIGHT

I leave Alice in the bedroom and return to the kitchen to find that my mother has made Mrs. Sarah Delano Cabot a cup of tea.

My dad has his arms crossed and is leaning against the counter. I can tell from the expression on his face he's doing everything he can to be polite to our guest.

"I guess you're asked this a lot—" he begins.

Mrs. Sarah Delano Cabot wearily raises a hand to cut him off. "I know. Yes, it *is quite tiresome,* but I *totally understand* your curiosity."

All this is said through a clenched jaw. I swear she hasn't unclenched since she got here. The words kind of ooze like syrup.

I remember that a lot of maple syrup comes from Maine.

Maybe there's a connection? Could be, but Alice doesn't talk like that.

Our guest goes on. "*Yes,* we are related to *those* Delanos. Franklin was a cousin of my grandfather."

Alice joins us. She has a backpack thrown over one shoulder.

"Oh, Mother, you're not boring them with family history again, are you?"

My mom's eyes are shining. She's absolutely captivated. I think at some level she would love to be able to say she was related to a famous president, instead of a pickle merchant who came here from Lithuania.

"It's not boring at all!" my mom insists. "I love to hear about other people's families. They're always so much more interesting than ours!"

Alice plops down onto the couch. She takes out a catalog with a picture of what looks like earnest young people on the cover from her backpack and starts to skim through it.

I recognize it immediately. It's a college catalog, meant to show why you should go to that school instead of any other. We had stacks of those lying around when Jake was applying. I looked at a few of them.

"Which one is that?" I ask.

"Barnard," Alice says, flipping through the pages of kids

walking around quads, staring at microscopes in labs, and performing in leotards.

"My brother applied to college last year," I say. "If you can tell the difference between the catalogs, you're a lot better than I am."

Alice leans toward me. "Actually, I think they're all the same. They just change the cover."

See? She's cool.

"Well, if that's the case, *darling,* why are you dragging me around the entire East Coast?" asks Mrs. Sarah Delano Clench. I mean Cabot.

"The catalogs are all the same," Alice explains, "but the schools aren't. Where's your brother going?"

"Cornell," I say, trying not to make it sound like a big deal.

Alice closes the catalog and looks up at me. "Wow! That's awesome!"

Cornell is hard to get into. I know that much.

"We're still deciding where we want to go," says her mother. She picks up a napkin and looks at it approvingly. "Cloth napkins. Very nice, Mrs. Kornberg."

Now it's my father's turn to clench his jaw. "It's Kantrowitz."

"I'm *so* sorry," Mrs. Sarah Delano All Jewish Last Names Sound Alike Cabot says. "It's just that we've been staying at so many places."

"I'm so happy you found us," Mom jumps in, changing the subject. "And on such short notice."

Before her mother can answer, Alice pipes up from the couch. "We had this other place all reserved, but then Mother spotted yours, and it's fifty dollars cheaper a night, so we're going to share a bed."

Mrs. Sarah Delano Cheapskate laughs. Well, I guess it's a laugh. It sounds more like a bark. "Alice is being *funny. Ha!* Isn't she a *stitch*? Yes, we did have somewhere else picked out, but your street looked so charming, we just had to stay here."

It turns out they're here to see Barnard and NYU. Alice seems really keen on coming to New York City to live.

"You should live in Brooklyn," I say. "All the cool people do."

Alice laughs. "Obviously. You live here."

"No, I mean—" I start.

"She's *teasing* you, young man. My goodness, Allie. I believe you've made him blush."

»«‹‹‹3+

Alice and her jerk mother go to dinner with some of her mother's "college chums" (I swear she actually used that phrase).

As soon as the door closes, my dad starts in. "I didn't know they still made them like that anymore."

"Well, I think she's very classy," my mom answers.

"She's like a character from a movie," I say.

My dad nods. "Exactly! I'm sure she's going to have a 'cocktail' with her 'college chums.'"

My mom makes sure not to make eye contact with me when she says, "Her daughter certainly seems nice. Doesn't she, Danny?"

"Mom!" I protest. "She's like five years older than me!"

Mom shakes her head. "I didn't mean it that way. You are so sensitive."

My dad clenches his jaw. "Yesss . . . ," he drawls. "You *Hebrew* people are so *emotional*."

It sounds just like Mrs. Sarah Delano Cabot. I burst out laughing, mostly because Mom is trying hard to be mad at Dad when I can tell she secretly agrees.

I figure I might as well try.

I clench my jaw and look down in my lap. "But, *Mother. Paper towels? Honestly,* where are the *linen napkins*?"

Dad gives me a high five and my mother throws a cloth napkin at me, hitting me in the face.

After dinner, I head to my room. I have homework for English and history and algebra. I am halfway through reading about the economic causes for the Revolutionary War when I hear noise outside. I guess the Cabots are back. There is a sharp rap on my door.

I get up and answer it. Mrs. Sarah Delano Cabot is standing there. Looking down her nose, of course.

"Good evening, Davis," she tries.

"Danny," I say.

"Yes, well," she goes on, "I just wanted to see if it was all right if Alice and I use the bathroom for a little bit."

I don't exactly know how to answer this. Like, what if I said no?

"Sure. Of course," I say. "You don't have to ask, you know."

Mrs. Sarah Delano Bathroom Hog clears her throat. "You never know about these things. I didn't want to inconvenience you."

I close my door and hear someone in the bathroom turning on the shower. I go back to reading.

It seems to take them forever to do whatever they are doing. I guess brushing teeth, hair, and whatever else people from Maine do in the bathroom.

There is a light tap on my door and Alice peers in.

She's wearing a freaking flannel nightgown. I was about to say something to the effect that it's the first time I've ever seen a girl in a flannel nightgown in real life and then I realize that, come to think of it, I've never seen a girl in any kind of pajamas in real life.

"It's all yours," Alice says. She looks around my room (which doesn't take too long) and her face falls. "Gosh. They stuck you in the closet? I hope we didn't kick you out of your room."

I sigh. "Nope. That was my brother's room. I've always just slept here." I know exactly what's coming.

"So . . . I guess that letter from Hogwarts never came, huh?" She says it like no one's *ever* thought of it before.

I laugh anyway. Because she's nice.

CHAPTER 28

WHERE IS MY LITTLE BOY?

I go to the bathroom and the first thing I notice is that the little bath soaps and shampoos that Mom put out are missing. I mean, they *are* for the guests, but I cannot believe that people with this much money would actually *take* them.

Unlike when Daan and Luuk stayed, there is no trace of anything from our guests in there. Even the wet towels have been removed. I can't explain why I find that so irritating.

I'm sure they didn't do it not to leave a mess. It's like Mrs. Sarah Delano Cabot doesn't trust me not to snoop in their toiletries or something. I guess I'm going to have to get used to all sorts of weird behavior from guests.

I take my shower (using *our* shampoo and soap) and towel

off and get into my sweatpants and T-shirt. I wonder if boys in Maine wear flannel pajamas like Alice's.

I head off to my room.

⊷⃪⃪◄ ◄ ◄ ⟨³⟩⊷

The next thing I know, someone is shaking me awake, and I freak out that I've overslept.

But even before I open my eyes, I can tell it's not Mom's hands.

These are more like talons, thin and with nails. And I know, with absolute certainty, that I'm not going to open my eyes and see my mother trilling, "Rise and shine!" I'm going to see something I don't want to. I clench my eyes shut harder.

Then the hissing noise starts. "Sss, sss!"

My eyes snap open even as I'm shrinking back, afraid of what might be waking me up with that terrible noise, with such a grip.

Staring at me through wild eyes is Mrs. Sarah Delano Cabot.

But she's totally not.

Her hair is sticking straight out, like she's been hit by static electricity. Her jaw is slack and her mouth dangles open.

But it's her eyes . . . her eyes . . .

They are wide open. The pupils are dilated, the size of dimes, and the color around them is a bright yellow. It's her eyes that make me yelp and struggle to get away from her, but she's got me locked tight.

"Chhh . . . ," she says, staring at me.

"Wh-what do you want?" I manage to gasp. She's skinny as anything, and it's totally freaking me out because how could this tiny lady have so much strength?

"What do you want from me?" I whisper, barely breathing.

"Yaaaa . . ." She is struggling to get a word out.

Her eyes close. She is concentrating.

And then . . .

I almost don't believe this myself, but I know what I see.

Mrs. Sarah Delano Cabot's iron grip relaxes, and slowly she begins to float, her feet no longer on the floor. She hangs there, and then her eyes pop open.

When she speaks, it's not in her low voice and New England accent.

It's the voice of a girl. With *some* sort of accent.

"Where is my little boy?" the voice screams. I swear to you I nearly peed. My parents didn't believe me, and now I'm going to be murdered by a horrible lady possessed by a vengeful ghost.

Whoever is inside Mrs. Delano Cabot lunges for me and I yell as loudly as I can, and I keep yelling even after she falls in a heap on the floor, because I am still terrified. This is so much worse than lights, than missing photos, than falling pictures.

I hear the pounding of footsteps outside my door and Alice appears, with my folks right behind her.

"Mother!" Alice gasps, and goes to her.

There isn't enough room in my closet for everyone. My folks stand in the doorway, looking confused.

"Danny, what is going on?" my mom asks.

I look down at my bedsheet, half expecting to see pee. I don't think anyone would blame me. But my bladder is clearly braver than I ever thought it would be. Braver than the rest of me, at least.

"Mom, she was acting crazy," I insist. "She shook me awake, and she yelled at me, and was, she was . . ." I struggle to find a word for "possessed and floating off the floor, *Ghostbusters*-style" that won't make me sound insane.

Mrs. Sarah Delano Cabot comes to and Alice hugs her. "Are you all right, Mother? What are you doing in Danny's room?" Her eyes are no longer wild, and she abruptly sits up, back straight. Immediately, she runs her fingers through her hair, arranging it neatly.

Her jaw is set again. "Why . . . I am *so sorry*. I have absolutely *no idea* how I got here."

"Were you sleepwalking? You scared Danny half to death! Mother, what did I tell you about taking that pill?"

"I never sleepwalk, I assure you," Mrs. Sarah Delano Cabot says sincerely to my parents. "Alice is right, it must have been that pill."

Alice turns to us. "Mother always has trouble sleeping in new places. The doctor prescribed this medication that has all sorts of side effects. I told her not to take it."

"I should have just asked you for a nightcap," Mrs. Sarah Delano Cabot says to my parents, smiling weakly, as Alice helps her to her feet.

"Are you sure she's all right?" my mom asks Alice. "We can call a doctor."

"Nonsense," Mrs. Sarah Delano Cabot says briskly. "I'm fine. Couldn't be better."

She straightens her back. "Again, I am *so sorry* to have inconvenienced everyone. Please forgive me."

With this she turns and marches back to Jake's bedroom.

Alice touches my arm, where her mother was just squeezing the life out of me. I flinch.

"Wow. You're really freaked," she says.

I can't help but laugh. "Yeah, what a shocker. Your mom wakes me in the middle of the night, talking in some weird voice, asking about your brother. Yeah, I'm a little freaked. Are you telling me that's totally normal up in Maine?"

"What brother?" Alice asks.

I feel the blood drain out of my face, and I get light-headed. I was *really* hoping that this whole episode was just the sleeping pill. I slowly turn to Alice. "Your mom shook me awake and then yelled, 'Where is my little boy?'"

"That's weird. . . . I don't have a brother. I have a sister."

"Maybe she was dreaming about her own brother?" my dad suggests.

Alice sits on my bed. Not next to me or anything. Just on the edge.

"She doesn't have a brother. I mean, she did, but he died when she was a little girl."

We all let that sink in for a minute.

"Alice, darling, are you coming to bed?" calls a voice from Jake's bedroom.

"Yes, Mother!" Alice answers. "Just a moment."

She turns to me. "My mom's just tired, that's all. Whatever she said, it was the medicine, I'm sure."

The next morning, there's a note for me on the kitchen counter. It's in perfect script, the kind we're supposed to learn in school but no one ever does anymore. The paper is thick and cream colored. It's the kind of stationery that costs a fortune. It even has a little design on the top linking the letters *S, D,* and *C.*

The note tells me that Mrs. Sarah Delano Cabot regrets terribly the incident of last night and hopes I will forgive her for interrupting my sleep. She and Alice will be gone all day, taking college tours. And then dinner with a distant cousin who works "in finance." But she hopes to see me tonight when they return. She signs it "With sincerest regards, I am Sarah Delano Cabot."

As if there was any doubt?

Who writes like this? It's like something out of a book.

I cannot wait to tell Nat and Gus about what happened. I text them. They're both busy after school, but they promise to get together with me tomorrow.

I want to text back that I hope I'm still in one piece tomorrow, but I know that's being a little dramatic.

At dinner, Dad entertains us with a reprise of his impression of Mrs. Sarah Delano Cabot, including a new bit where he's trying to get a piece of chicken into his mouth but his jaw won't unclench.

"Why, this is so *embarrassing*," he says. "I *must* write a letter of apology to the chicken."

I have to say, my dad can be pretty funny sometimes.

I look at my mom, who has gotten a case of the giggles. I love that my dad can still make her laugh like that.

To my relief, there is no return visit that night. I learn later that Mrs. Sarah Demonic Possession and her daughter stayed at her cousin's so late, they slept there.

The next morning, I'm in my room when there's a soft knock on the door.

I open it to see Alice, in her lacrosse jacket, with her and her mom's suitcases.

"Hey," I say.

She smiles. "Hey yourself."

"How were your tours?" I ask. I think it's pretty impressive that I can speak to a high school senior without sounding like an idiot. Though I admit, I did come up with that question yesterday afternoon just in case Alice talked to me again.

"They were . . . okay," she answers. "The tour guide at NYU kept going on and on about politics, which is important, but it would have been nice to hear more about the academics."

I nod. "Totally." That seems like a thing a guy her age would say. I am trying to keep up here. I don't have much left.

"So my mom wants to see you," she says.

"Um, sure. You know why?"

Alice shrugs. "I think she just wants to make sure you're okay. She freaked you out pretty badly the other night."

"Totally." Now I have just gone into idiot mode. "I mean, not that bad." I think if Alice had said "Would you put your head in the toilet and flush?" I would have nodded and said "Totally."

I escape and walk down the hallway. Before I knock on the door to Jake's room, I hear humming from inside. It's not a song I recognize, but somehow I know it. It's from another country, like a folk tune or a lullaby.

I knock on the door and am told to come in.

Mrs. Sarah Delano Cabot is at the desk, her back turned to me.

"Danny, I did want to see you before we go," she says.

I nod and am about to say "Totally" when I stop myself.

"I feel just *dreadful* about our little rendezvous the other night. I *do* hope I didn't frighten you too much."

"Nope, it was fine," I lie. "Just surprised me, that's all."

Mrs. Sarah Delano Cabot barks a laugh. "I should think so!"

She gets up and shakes my hand firmly. "You take care of yourself, young man!"

As she heads out the door, my curiosity gets the better of me.

"If you don't mind," I say, "what was the name of the tune you were humming before I came in the room?"

Another barking laugh. "I beg your pardon?"

"I heard you humming before I knocked on the door."

"Oh, no!" Mrs. Sarah Delano Cabot sniffs. "I can't carry a tune to *save my life*. Ask Alice. You'll never hear *me* humming!"

CHAPTER 29

THINGS THAT GO MOO IN THE NIGHT

"If you hum that one more time, I swear I'm gonna throw you in the freezer," grouses Gus.

I've already hummed the tune for my mom and dad, who have no idea what it is. It's driving me crazy, because it's so familiar, but I have no idea where I heard it. I was hoping maybe we sang it in kindergarten or something, but Nat and Gus clearly don't know it either.

We're walking Gus to Baublitz's—his dad has sprung an unexpected shift at the store on him. He's in a lousy mood and I can't blame him. It's not like he *wants* to work there. Unlike Nat, Gus is expected to help out, and even worse, his father has made it clear that he's going to take over the business one day, and that's how it is.

Nat tries to be supportive. Like her dad before her, she's been told all her life that it's her choice if she wants to work at the store, that she can be whatever she wants. So if she wants to be a doctor, she can.

But Gustave Baublitz is going to be a butcher because Baublitzes have been butchering meat in Brooklyn since 1915, and some traditions are too powerful to simply walk away from.

"It would break my dad's heart," Gus says. "Besides, it's nice to be part of history. Like being Prince William or something. It's my inheritance."

I don't mention that Prince William probably doesn't have to spend his whole day in a bloody apron chopping up animal parts, but then again, Gus's dad, Emil, is kind of like royalty in the neighborhood. He knows everyone's order, just like Sammy. And Joe.

Emil grew up in the neighborhood and has watched it change and grow. He began stocking fancier cuts of meat as his clientele started asking for them. Sure, people can buy meat at the supermarket or at expensive stores like Whole Foods, but a lot of them still love the idea of the neighborhood butcher.

"You're doing it again," Gus says.

I didn't even realize I was humming. "Sorry," I say.

Nat tugs at the straps on her backpack. It looks heavier

than usual, which is saying something since she's always got books in there to read. "It sounds like it *is* some song, but I don't know what."

She looks at me. "Was that Mrs. Sarah What's-Her-Face the kind of lady who would do something like that for a joke? You know, to weird you out?"

"First of all, I don't think she's ever made a joke in her life," I say. "And second of all, that thing the night before was weird enough."

Gus takes three pieces of gum out of his pocket and pops them in his mouth. "Phoo gurgle abow—"

"Gus, for crying out loud, *chew first!*" Nat exclaims. "You are totally grossing us out here."

She and I watch Gus's jaw working furiously to wrestle the gum into submission. Not a pretty picture, I can tell you.

Finally he is able to push the wad into his cheek and he tries again. "You sure about that floating part? I mean, that's some total special effects movie stuff there."

"I'm not sure of *anything* anymore," I blurt out. "I know there's no such thing as ghosts. I mean, I *used* to know that. I want to think there's another explanation for this."

Nat, logical as ever, sighs. "Danny, I just don't get why this is happening *now.*"

"I know," I say. "Part of me is wondering if it's all in my head."

"But that lady showing up in your room wasn't in your

head," Gus protests. "If it was me, I would have screamed my head off."

"I pretty much did, to be honest."

"Who knows, Gus?" Nat says. "Maybe one night *you'll* be haunted by the ghosts of the animals you've killed! Think about it. . . . You'll be asleep in your bed"—I lean in and continue—"and somewhere in the distance you hear . . . a forlorn noise. . . ."

Nat covers her mouth and emits a low, spectral sound. "Moo . . . moo . . ."

"Oh no! Ghost cow!" Gus calls out, backing away from us. "And it won't stop until I become vegetarian!"

We all crack up.

"Nat, just remember," Gus says, suddenly turning serious before we go into the butcher shop. "We don't kill them. Okay?"

Gus is very sensitive about this. They buy the sides of beef, the chickens, and the pigs from small family farms in upstate New York.

"When I was your age, I'd already killed a pig all by myself!" Gus's grandfather yells from behind the stoop. He pops up with a broom in one hand. "What do you think a butcher is, anyway?"

I look in the store window. Hanging there is a bunch of meat on hooks. With its hammered tin ceiling and big glass cases filled with steaks, sausages, chicken breasts, and that kind of thing, the place still looks pretty much like it did back in the days when Old Man Baublitz *was* Gus's age. There's still sawdust on the beautifully tiled floor, which is used to soak up the blood (that's what Gus told us), but now it mostly makes the place feel old-timey. Other, fancier butcher stores have opened in the neighborhood recently, and they've bought all this stuff to try to *look* like they've been here forever, but once you walk into Baublitz Butcher Shop you feel like you've really walked back into history. They've even kept the old phone booth in the back. There's no phone anymore, but it's a cool place to sit while you're waiting for your order.

The new families who come into the store don't really want to think about where their meat comes from. They could get their meat from a grocery store, but they want the best. So they trust that Gus's family picks the finest cuts, and they happily pay top dollar to take home their meat wrapped up in waxed paper, "just like the old days."

Emil is a nice-looking guy, with a head of thick jet-black hair, and usually a paper hat perched on top of it. Like everything else here, the hat is traditional, like the ones you see on butchers in old children's books.

"Best-looking boy in the neighborhood," Old Man Baublitz says. "Plenty of girls. Always." He jerks his thumb at Gus. "So how come this one turned out lookin' like a pig's butt?"

He turns to Emil. "Guess the mailman was an ugly son of a gun!" Then he just about busts a gut laughing.

Gus bites his lip. He knows he has to keep his mouth

shut, because he's supposed to respect his grandpa, but if it was me, I'd say something. With all due respect, Old Man Baublitz isn't exactly God's gift to women, if you know what I mean.

"Leave the kid alone, Pop," Emil says.

"Hey, I was just busting his chops," protests the old man. "Jeez, so sensitive."

This is how old people talk in Brooklyn. Still.

"You're a handsome boy. Don't listen to him," a woman with a stroller says to Gus, who blushes bright red.

He turns to Nat with his eyebrows raised. "Don't ask me," she says quickly. "But speaking objectively, chewing like five pieces of gum at one time does not make you particularly attractive to the opposite sex."

Gus blows a bubble. "It was three. And why are you making assumptions? I could be gay."

Nat raises one eyebrow. "Believe me, no one of any gender is going to want to look at that."

Gus blows an even bigger bubble. "Says you!"

"You're drooling," I observe.

Gus wipes his mouth with his sleeve.

"You guys can wait outside until I finish Mrs. Rubin's order," Emil says.

We head outside and sit on the narrow stoop of the apartment entrance nestled between the shops on Court Street. Nat slips off her backpack and it lands with a thud.

"So what have you got in there?" Gus asks. "The entire Brooklyn Public Library?"

Nat undoes the strap. "Just part of it."

She empties the contents onto my lap.

About ten books slide out. I read a few titles. *Best Ghost Stories. The Scariest Tales Ever Told. The Horror Hall of Fame.*

"Research," Nat says simply.

CHAPTER 30

OLIVER ONIONS?

As I look at the pile of books, I feel something loosen in my chest. It's like I've been wound up tight ever since these things started happening and I haven't even noticed.

"So . . . you *do* believe me?" I say.

Nat picks up one of the books. "Look, I'm not saying your apartment is haunted, but . . ."

Gus takes a deep breath. "But it's a possibility."

"Maybe we can find out what's really happening when these things occur," Nat says.

"Like maybe there's something causing people to have hallucinations?" I ask. "Because I'm not the only one who's been seeing things, you know."

"Most of which had logical explanations," Nat counters.

I hate it when she makes sense.

"Only *you* heard the humming and saw the lights going on and off."

Gus is looking at the books uneasily. "So . . . *you're* going to read all of these, right? And tell us what you've learned?"

"Wrong," Nat says. "*We're* going to read them. We'll split them up."

Gus groans. "This is sounding more and more like homework."

I grab one from the pile. I read the title out loud. *"The Collected Ghost Stories of Oliver Onions."*

Gus bursts out laughing. "No way! That cannot be his real name. What is he, like a circus clown?"

I take a look at the serious-faced man on the cover. "I don't think so. And anyway, clowns are freaking scary, so let's not go there."

Nat grabs the book impatiently. "He happens to be one of the most famous ghost story writers ever. I spent a whole afternoon at the library looking this stuff up."

Gus brightens. "Hey! I know. I can look on the Internet. And you guys can read the books."

I know what that means. Gus will take two minutes doing an online search and then spend the rest of the time playing games.

"I've already looked on the Internet," Nat says. "There's a whole lot of stuff, but mostly it's people going into dark houses and using weird machines to detect the presence of ectoplasm or whatever." She clearly doesn't believe that sort of thing is valuable.

"So nothing about what to do if your apartment is haunted?" I ask. I can't believe I didn't bother to check this out myself.

"For the most part, the sites I went to tend to think that either people are imagining things or that there's some other explanation," Nat says.

"Hey! Lazybones! Quit hanging outside wit' your friends!" Old Man Baublitz yells to Gus.

"Dad said he was going to call me when Mrs. Rubin left," Gus answers.

Emil is at the door with a broom. "She left about five minutes ago."

"So why didn't you call me?" Gus asks.

Emil sighs. I think he knows Gus really doesn't want to be a butcher. "I guess I was hoping you'd take some initiative."

Emil stretches and turns to me. "So, how's your folks, Danny? Your dad still working on that film?"

"Not right now," I say.

Emil smiles. "I remember he used to talk about it all the time. It sounded great. He doesn't talk about it much anymore."

"Yeah," I say, not knowing what else to add.

Emil hands the broom to Gus and sees the books. He bends down and picks one up. "So who's into ghost stories? I used to love them when I was a kid."

"Really?" says Gus. "Danny's been having all sorts of weird things happening in his apartment, right?"

Emil's eyes brighten. "Yeah? Like what?"

I can see that as long as I'm telling Emil about the apartment, Gus won't have to sweep. So I go through all that's happened: the knocking on the door and the lights going on and off and Mrs. Sarah Delano Cabot's unscheduled appearance in my bedroom.

Emil is rapt. He rubs his jaw a few times and mutters a curse word under his breath. Then his eyes narrow.

"You making this up, Danny?"

"No, I swear. Why would I?" I protest.

"Seems like you wanted that room pretty bad," Emil says.

Nat begins to gather up the books. "I thought that too at first. But there are too many things that other people saw too."

Gus turns to Emil. "You ever seen a ghost, Dad?"

"Don't be stupid, Gus," his dad snaps. He stares back into the shop.

"What about Grandpa?" Gus asks excitedly.

Emil shrugs. "Your grandmother said it was 'cause he'd been out on a drunk all night, but he always swears that didn't matter."

"Hey, *Pop*!" Emil calls into the store.

There's some shuffling and Old Man Baublitz comes out, wiping his hands on his apron. "Jeez," he mutters. "Guess I'm the only one around here workin' today, huh? You boys enjoying the sunshine?"

Emil ignores him. "I was just tellin' the kids about when you saw that ghost."

CHAPTER 31

OLD MAN BAUBLITZ TELLS A TALE

Gus looks annoyed. "How come you never told me the story before?"

The old man laughs. "Your grandma would have hung me up in the window if I had. When I told your dad he didn't sleep for a week."

We turn to Emil. "Pop, don't exaggerate," he says. "It was one night."

Gus is impatient. "So what was the story?"

"This must have been about 'fifty-five or 'fifty-six," the old man begins, and Emil sighs and goes back into the shop. "I'd just gotten out of the service. I know it wasn't 'fifty-seven be-cause that's when the Dodgers left Brooklyn for Los Angeles. The lousy stinkin' bums. After all we done for them. Rooting all those years. And then they up and leave us. I tell ya—"

It's hard to explain to someone not from Brooklyn what it meant to folks who were around back then when our baseball team moved. My grandmother always says, "It was like they pulled my father's heart from his body, I swear. That man was never the same."

"So it was after you left the army," Nat says patiently, trying to get the train back on track.

"Right. So I'm walking up Hicks Street, you know, near the fire station? In those days there were still lots of bars around there, with lots of cheap booze for the sailors and the guys who worked loading and paintin' ships at the docks, you know?"

Gus brightens when he hears his dad start sweeping in the shop.

Gus nods. "Yeah, go on, Grandpa. Take your time."

"So I'm feeling pretty good, having had a few, but not so much that I'm in my cups," the old man says. I marvel at how many ways these old guys have for saying they were drunk. "It's dark, but I see this young woman standin' in the doorway of one of the carriage houses—you know, the ones with the round windows?"

We all know which ones he means. In the old days, a lot of them were boardinghouses.

"So here's the thing. She's dressed funny. I mean, she looks like a young woman, but she's dressed like someone from the war. You know, the one in Europe."

"So she was dressed in old clothes," Nat says.

The old man nods. He looks like he's seeing her again right now. "She was real pretty, but sad-lookin' too. All pale, with dark circles under her eyes."

We kids exchange glances. This is getting good.

"She calls out to me, 'Hey, mister! Got a minute?' Now, don't get the wrong idea. I was already dating your grandmother, so I wasn't about to be doing anything with no tramp. She was speakin' with some type of accent. I could tell she wasn't from here. I try to keep walkin', but she reaches out and grabs my arm."

Emil has stopped sweeping and stands in the doorway, listening.

The old man can see we're hooked. He leans in. We lean in. Emil leans in.

"So I'm about to tell her I ain't interested, when she pulls out a rope and asks me if I could tie a slipknot. She says she don't know how."

The old man takes a swig of coffee.

"So what did you do?" demands Gus.

The old man shoots him a look. "I was gonna beat it, but she was clutchin' my arm so tight and the look on her face was so pitiful. So I said, 'Sure, I can do that. No problem.'"

A customer pushes past us and goes into the store. Emil gestures to one of the guys who works there to help the customer. No way he's missing this.

"I make the knot in the rope and hand it back to her. She looks so happy. 'Thank you, sir. Thank you, Thank you!' It was a little weird how thrilled she was with it, but I thought, Okay, lady. Whatever floats your boat, you know? She goes back inside without even a good night, and I head home."

The Old Man sits back and looks at us, nodding.

"That's it?" asks Gus incredulously.

Emil smacks him on the back of his head. "No, that's not it, you dope. Let your grandfather finish."

I look at the Old Man, trying to imagine him as a young man, weaving his way through the Heights. His voice is now barely a whisper. "So I don't think much of it, until a few days later. I'm walking by the same house on the way home for lunch. You know how in those days your grandma and me lived on Henry Street? I don't think you ever saw that place—"

"Dad!" Emil prods him.

"Oh, right. So I'm walking by that place and I see a different lady out front, watering the plants in her window box. I'm curious, so I ask her about the woman with the rope."

Another customer comes into the shop. Emil looks worried. A few more and he'll have to miss the end of the story.

"Come on, Pop," he pleads.

"So . . . *she* says, 'What woman?' Nobody's living there but her and her husband."

Nat is clutching a book to her chest so hard I'm surprised

she can breathe. Gus is still holding a piece of gum he un-wrapped five minutes ago.

"Then a strange look comes over her. She asks me to describe the woman. I tell her what she looked like and she goes and gets her husband. He's my age. She says to me, 'Tell him about the woman,' and I do, and I think he's gonna faint right then and there. I ask what's the problem and this is what he tells me."

None of us moves. Not even Emil. People push past him to get into the store.

"When the guy was a kid during the war, the army sent this lady to stay with his family, 'cause they were renting out rooms. She was real quiet, from Germany. Never talked to anyone. Just sat in a chair all day, smoking cigarettes. He would run errands for her, getting her stuff to eat, like that. His parents would leave it for her in her room, and she'd barely touch it.

"One day she's visited by a bunch of guys who say they're from the government. It turns out in Germany she was a double agent working against the Nazis. I guess the gestapo found out and tortured her pretty bad. But some of our spies got her out and were keeping her safe here in Brooklyn, try-ing to get what information they could out of her.

"After the government guys leave, she calls for the boy to get her something. She has a list and one of the things on it is rope. She asks him if he knows how to tie knots. He was pretty proud of himself, being a Boy Scout, and showed her all sorts of knots, plus the ones the sailors down at the navy yard taught him. She's all interested and asks him to tie her a slipknot. He does, and she thanks him."

The old man pauses one last time. He sure knows how to tell a story. He should be in one of these books Nat checked out.

"That night the woman is all happy. First time they see her smile. The next morning, the kid's mother goes up to get her for breakfast and finds her. She'd hanged herself with the rope.

"And that night I walked by? It was ten years to the day she'd done it."

CHAPTER 32

WHO YOU GONNA CALL?

The old man looks pretty pleased with himself. He heads back into the shop. "Next customer!" he sings gaily. Like he didn't just scare the freaking life out of us.

Gus shivers. "Jeez, that was creepy as—"

Nat cuts him off. "Your grandpa tells a good story. But it has nothing to do with Danny." She picks out three books and hands them to me. They're all anthologies of ghost stories.

I look at them skeptically. "You sure this is a good idea?"

"What's the problem?" she asks impatiently.

"I'm just . . . I dunno, I guess I'm afraid if I read too many of these, I'll, you know, get ideas?"

"So it *is* all in your head!" Nat says triumphantly. "You admit it!"

I grab the books. "I'm just jumpy enough as it is. This might make it that much worse."

"Hey!" Gus has that look on his face he gets when he has one of his ideas.

Nat's shoulders sag. "Yes, Gus?"

Gus's eyes are shining. This is going to be good. "How about that lady on Montague Street?"

"You mean the psychic?" asks Nat.

"Yeah!" Gus says. "I bet she'd be able to help."

I'm trying to think of a diplomatic way to tell Gus what a ridiculous idea this is. I give up. "That's a ridiculous idea. She's totally bogus."

Gus's face falls. "How do *you* know?"

"Don't you remember when Luis's aunt had that whole thing with her?" Nat says.

"What thing?" Gus asks.

"You know . . ." I pick up the story. We all know it. Luis is in our class. "She went to that woman because she wanted to know if her husband was fooling around. The woman made her give her 'gifts' and money and all sorts of things so she could get in touch with the spirit world. Luis said it turned out to be a total con. They called the cops on her and everything."

Gus won't admit defeat. It's kind of admirable in a way. And also irritating. "Yeah, but that was different. This one is about a *ghost*."

"Let it go," Nat says. "We're not using her. She's going to ask for money, and we don't have it."

"How about those guys on the Internet?" Gus will not let anything go.

"How about not?" I say. "You think my parents are going to let a bunch of strangers post videos of our apartment on the Internet? And what do you think the chances are of anyone renting the room if they think it's haunted?"

"We have to prove this ourselves," Nat says, then adds quickly, "If there is anything to prove, of course."

"Other than that I'm nuts," I grumble.

"That's it!" Gus says.

This is going to be good.

"Okay, Mr. Ghostbuster," Nat says. "What is it?"

"Danny just needs *proof*," Gus says. "Like a photograph or something."

I pretend to faint on the street. "I cannot believe it. History was made today."

Gus lifts me up. "What are you talking about?"

"You actually came up with something useful," I tell him.

I can see that Gus is trying to decide whether I'm actually giving him a compliment or busting his chops like the old man.

"I did?" he says.

Nat nods. "Yes! That's actually a smart thing to say."

"Remember Katia the dog walker who took those photos of our apartment? The ones she said showed what she assumed was my face reflecting in the window? What if it wasn't?" I ask.

Nat looks at me. "We need to see those pictures."

I agree. "I'm sure my mom has her email."

There is a line of people coming to pick up their orders, as it's getting close to dinnertime. Emil waves from behind the counter.

Gus grabs the slimmest volume of ghost stories and heads inside. "Catch me up later!"

I promise to text if anything happens before school tomorrow.

I walk Nat to Haddad's. She usually stays there and does homework in the back until her dad finishes work and then goes home with him. We pass all the other Middle Eastern stores, the hookah bar, the clothing store with the hijabs in the window, the bakery with lots of pastries.

Most of these stores are packed with men and women speaking Arabic, families shopping for the foods from their home countries, the places they left when they came here looking for a new life, just like my Jewish great-grandparents.

"When's your next guest?" Nat asks.

I bite my lip. I sure don't want another visit. "I think it's next week. Two girls from Japan. I don't think they speak a lot of English."

"So you shouldn't have to worry until then, right? I mean,

since you've started having guests, the weird things only seem to happen when they're there."

I think about this. "Yeah . . . I mean, maybe. I guess it depends whether all the other stuff from before—like the camera—or during—like the picture frame—can be explained some other way."

Nat tries to look encouraging. "Probably. And I bet there's an explanation for all this. We just haven't thought of it yet."

"Like on *Scooby-Doo*," I say. "Somebody's trying to scare me and then we'll trap the monster and pull the mask off."

Nat laughs. "It'll turn out to be your landlord, who's trying to sell the building."

"That's too predictable," I say. "What about Mrs. Sarah Delano Cabot? She found out there's a fortune's worth of diamonds buried in the walls. So she set the whole thing up."

We've arrived at Haddad's. Of course Sammy is deep in conversation with some old customer who's rolling her eyes in ecstasy tasting a sample of whatever cheese or olive or other delicacy he's given her.

Nat squeezes my hand. I guess she wants me to not be afraid. "Yeah, Danny, no. I just think at the end of all this we'll feel foolish that we thought for a minute that room was really haunted."

I desperately want to believe her.

CHAPTER 33

HORROR STORIES

I go home, burdened with the two heavy books Nat gave me to read and the thoughts filling my head. Of course she's right. But the thing bothering me is that sure, there seems to be an explanation for each of the weird things that happened, but no *one* explanation for all of them, and for all of them happening in the same couple of weeks. Each event has its own logical explanation, but why so many?

After dinner—during which Mom went on and on about how excited she was to have Japanese tourists staying with us, and wondering what they would want for breakfast, and my dad wearily suggesting that maybe they already figured out what they want to do on their own, and my mom testily answering that *maybe* they won't know everything and we could at least have authentic bagels for them—I think I've gotten a little off track. Sorry. After dinner, I went to my room and took out the smaller of the two books.

It was an anthology called *The Best Ghost Stories Ever.* I hate titles like that. They sound like those commercials on the TV shows my grandma watches that promise to seal any leak or the microwave gizmo that will bring back the "just cooked" flavor to any leftover. I wanted there to be a sentence after the first story that said "But wait! There's more!"

So I read the stories, and take my word for it, they were *not* the scariest ghost stories ever. I mean, they were well written and everything, but not anywhere near as creepy as what was happening to me. Or even what Sammy or Joe or Old Man Baublitz told us.

First off, if you're going to spend the night in a spooky old abandoned house (is there any other kind?) where someone was murdered years ago, what do you *think* is going to happen? Or if you take some jewel or mummy's hand from a tomb or crypt, are you *really* surprised when someone from "beyond the grave" comes and wants it back?

A whole lot of stories were about people doing something terrible like committing murder or cheating someone, and then the person they killed or wronged comes back and haunts them—or maybe it's just their own guilty conscience that drives them nuts and makes them imagine things.

That got me thinking. Have *I* done anything terrible to someone who died? I tried to remember. The only thing I could think of was when I got mad at Adam Scheinman in third grade and deliberately hit him in the head while we were playing dodgeball.

But Adam Scheinman didn't die (although he acted like he was going to—jeez, he should have won an award for that performance). He just never forgave me. I saw him at a bar mitzvah last year and he told me he still can't hear well out of his right ear. I told him I didn't even hit his ear, it was his forehead. I guess he heard that fine because he made some crack about my wearing sneakers to a bar mitzvah because I couldn't afford dress shoes. Which was total garbage, but I let it go because I am a better person than he is.

Okay, really? I only let it go because I am a head taller than him now (he's *really* short) and it would look bad if I hit him.

I seriously couldn't think of another person I had wronged. I'm just a kid, after all. Who would haunt me?

Then there was a story about people renovating houses and disturbing the spirits of the dead people who used to live there.

I sat up. Wait. We *did* renovate Jake's room. I mean, we didn't take out a wall and find someone's bones or anything, but we did paint it and put new furniture in it. Maybe some spirit doesn't like Ikea?

I yawned and put the book down. That was enough for one night. Actually, it made me less and less convinced that something was really going on. The more stories I read, the more it seemed unlikely that there were supernatural happenings. It *had* to be my disappointment pushing me to see things that weren't there.

I headed to the bathroom for a shower, happy that I could lock the door and chill out in peace, knowing that I'd be left alone for at least a day or two before our guests arrived.

I took a nice hot shower, feeling all the craziness of the past few weeks wash off me.

The bathroom filled with steam. After my shower I sat on the toilet seat with my feet up, my eyes closed, pretending I was at a spa, in a steam room.

I usually sit in there until my folks yell at me to come out and go to bed. I opened my eyes and stared at the medicine cabinet.

The mirror was all steamed up.

But it was clear as anything.

Someone had taken their finger and written a message on it.

In spidery, old-fashioned letters was scrawled:

Where is my little boy?

CHAPTER 34

GOING DOWN TO DUMBO

Yes, of course I checked to make sure the door was locked. I guess someone could have used a credit card to pop the lock and come in without me hearing, but who? My parents? They can be pretty goofy, but there's no way they'd do that.

I was late for school today—having gotten very little sleep, of course. I have math first period and then science, so I can't talk to Nat and Gus until lunchtime. As usual, Gus has homework to do that he should have finished last night, so he's kind of distracted, and Nat doesn't understand why I didn't take a photo of the mirror.

"I don't bring my phone in the bathroom with me when I take a shower," I explain. "And once I opened the door, the cold air made the steam go away. So the message got all runny."

Nat takes a bite of her falafel sandwich. It was made that morning, so it's delicious, the crunchy falafel covered with the perfect amount of tangy white tahini sauce. Nat always brings one for me, because Sammy knows how much I love it and gives her extra. "Are you *sure* it said that?"

"I know what I read," I say. "What are you suggesting?"

I make the mistake of waving my sandwich for emphasis near Gus. He leans in and takes a ginormous bite. He's already had lunch, but that doesn't seem to matter.

Gus chews and swallows thoughtfully before offering an opinion. "Sometimes you *think* you see things in steamy mirrors. Like once I swear I saw the words 'fungus mania.'"

"What does that even mean?" I ask.

Gus shrugs and wipes his mouth on his sleeve. "You got me. What does 'Where is my little boy?' mean?"

Nat closes her eyes. "I can't even. Gus, sometimes . . ."

Gus grins. "Let me guess, sometimes you dream about me."

"Only about killing you," Nat says. "Can we concentrate on Danny's ghost?"

"So you really think it's real?"

Nat pulls out a notebook from her backpack. Naturally she took notes on the ghost stories she read, something I should have done. "I put them in different categories. It seems to me if there *is* someone, it's a restless spirit that's been disturbed."

"That's what I thought!" I say excitedly. "Like maybe we

threw something out from Jake's room by mistake when we were fixing it up."

Nat nods. "So can you think of anything? Like an old doll or something?"

I laugh. "Oh, *right*. Jake had an old doll lying around his room and our mom just threw it out."

"Look, we don't even know it's a ghost," Gus says. "It could be a demon, right? I saw a video online about these demon hunters, and—"

"Were they in Brooklyn?" I ask.

"Um, I think they were like in eastern Europe some-where," Gus says.

"I don't want to hear about any eastern European demon-hunter garbage," Nat snaps. "We're in Brooklyn. I just have a feeling this is someone who was unhappy while they were alive."

"Like that German spy ghost?" I ask.

We fall silent. That was a really creepy story.

I remember something. "Oh, yeah. I finally heard from Katia. She says we can go by her workspace this afternoon."

The bells rings. Five minutes to get to our next class. We agree to meet outside as soon as school is over.

It turns out Katia's place is all the way down on Jay Street, closer to the water. It's about a fifteen-minute walk from school. Like so much of Brooklyn, this area has gone through a lot of changes. In the old days, it was all warehouses, but once the ships stopped pulling in, a lot of the empty floors were rented by artists.

Then someone had the bright idea to convert all the loft spaces and old warehouses into luxury buildings, and what used to be called "the waterfront" got a new name. They do that a lot around here. The areas called Red Hook and South Brooklyn had reputations for being unsafe, so some real estate big shots chopped off a part of that and called it Cobble Hill and it sounded a lot classier.

Since this place is right under where the Manhattan Bridge hits Brooklyn, somebody decided on "Down Under the Manhattan Bridge Overpass" and shortened it to Dumbo. That's what it's been called pretty much since I've been alive.

By now most of Dumbo has become expensive apartments and fancy boutiques and restaurants. But on the fringes, like where Katia has her studio, there are still some funky spaces that haven't been totally converted yet.

We get to the address, a big old building with doors covered in peeling rusty orange paint. The only things that look new are the names next to the buzzers. There are all sorts of small businesses, like a dress designer and an architecture firm, and people like Katia who share an office with other people.

Katia buzzes us in and we enter the giant elevator, which slowly creaks its way up to the eighth floor. I assume the elevator goes back to the days when people had to move all sorts of things in and out to trucks waiting to deliver goods all over the city, or maybe even all over the country. Those days are long gone. There are no more goods to move.

The elevator takes forever to settle, groaning and complaining like an old man getting comfortable on a couch, and finally the doors open.

We're greeted with a confusing set of hallways leading off in all directions. Nat peers at the various arrows pointing the way to different offices, and then we head down a long dusty corridor.

It feels like we've walked two city blocks before we finally arrive at Katia's place. There are stickers on the door, some of rock bands from the eighties that my parents still listen to, some of anime and manga.

The door opens and Katia welcomes us in. "Okay, Ghostbusters, let's get to work!"

CHAPTER 35

PHOTO FINISH

Katia shares the space with two other photographers. One of them is there, a tall older guy with swept-back hair. He's got a light set up on a table and is carefully positioning a bracelet on a black velvet backing.

"He takes all the pictures for one of the big jewelry store's ads," Katia informs us.

"I always wondered how they made them look so good," Gus marvels as we watch the guy positioning like half a dozen different lights at different heights, and keep running back to his camera to check on how it looks. He smiles.

"Yeah, this is why they pay me the big bucks," he says.

Katia pulls us away. "He's one of the best. I couldn't do that all day, but he loves it."

The third photographer apparently does weddings. We

pass her area, and there are giant photos of happy couples, all looking pretty much the same and posing with the Brooklyn Bridge behind them, the same place you see in car ads whenever there's a car displayed with the Manhattan skyline in the background. I've been down here on weekends in the summer and I swear there's literally a line of brides and grooms waiting their turn to get their photos taken.

"Do you ever do weddings?" Nat asks Katia.

Katia laughs. "Me? Not a chance. Those brides are killers. If you miss *one* picture, they scream you've ruined their wedding."

"That's true," Gus muses. "I remember my cousin Clara. The photographer didn't get a picture of her sister and her with their grandmother. And she always brings it up whenever she shows her pictures. And that was like ten years ago."

"Yeah, totally," says Katia.

We get to her area. It's messy but cool. She has posters up of bands she's photographed, and some headshots of actors. I don't recognize any of them.

Katia sweeps an arm up and points to the wall near the window. "My pet project," she announces.

The wall is plastered with enormous portraits of dogs of all sizes lit like movie stars. They look very glamorous. And also really funny.

"*Pet* project, I get it!" Gus says. "Are these the dogs you walk?"

"Some of them," Katia replies. "And some are just dogs I like. You can see pretty much every kind of dog in Brooklyn."

Nat goes up to the photos and examines them. "They're beautiful."

Katia gives a little smile. "Thanks. I'm hoping to get a gallery interested in them someday." She brightens. "Hey! Maybe if there *is* a ghost I can use it for publicity!"

She turns to her computer. It's like my dad's, with a giant monitor. She clicks a few keys and the finder comes up.

Katia peers at the screen. "Let's see. . . . I photographed your place in late August, right? Here you are."

She clicks the mouse and a series of pictures of our apartment comes up. She scrolls through the various shots. There are photos of the outside of the building and our hallway, the views from our windows, our kitchen, and the bedroom.

"These are the ones I sent to your mom," she announces. "I need to find the originals, before I removed the face."

I shiver a little when she says that.

Katia clicks on another folder. These appear to be the photos she's looking for. She nods in satisfaction. "Bingo!" She clicks on one image and opens it.

It's Jake's bedroom, clean and in guest-ready shape.

Even at this size, it's clear there's something in the window.

I can feel Nat and Gus holding their breath as Katia zooms in.

A face fills the screen. It's hard to see much, though, because it seems to be glowing.

"Wait, I can make it better," Katia says as she fiddles with a few sliders in the software, changing the contrast and sharpness so that the features become clearer.

And then we see it.

A long, narrow face, black hair parted in the middle. Sad dark eyes, and a long curved nose. A mouth set in what looks like a permanent expression of grief. She wears a black dress with a white lace collar.

A shiver goes through me as the face stares back at us from the past.

"Who are you?" Nat asks in barely a whisper.

"And where is your little boy?" I wonder out loud.

CHAPTER 36

THE PAST IS PRESENT

As we leave Katia's, the sun is already going down, creating broad dark shadows between the tall buildings we pass.

With the Manhattan Bridge looming over us, and the cobblestoned streets under our feet, this part of Dumbo feels particularly eerie. The warehouse interiors may be converted into luxury apartments filled with rich tenants, but the outsides are untouched, so it's easy to feel pulled back to the days of horse-drawn carriages and ships carrying cargo into the ports. Maybe all of Brooklyn is filled with ghosts: shades of great ships still pulling into the navy yard, old mom-and-pop stores haunting the shiny new chain stores that replaced them.

I half expect to see a sad-eyed girl in a lace collar pop out from around a corner, but there are just groups of tourists heading to the entrance to the Brooklyn Bridge or maybe to one of the gourmet bakeries. It's a relief to be brought back to the present.

I realize none of us has spoken since we got on the old elevator to leave. On the way down, the rusty moans and shrieks sure seemed a whole lot creepier.

Finally, Nat turns to me. "So . . . what's our next step? I mean, assuming the girl in the window is the one who's been bothering you."

"Oh, you *think*?" Gus asks. "Or maybe it's a coincidence. Maybe she was the window washer . . . because you know window washers tend to wear lace collars."

Nat glares at Gus. "Sometimes you can be such a jerk."

"All I'm saying is that *of course* that's the girl," Gus snaps.

We've made it to Vinegar Hill. This is a long high walk that takes you up from Dumbo to the northern part of the Heights. As we walk, the joyous barks and yips from the dog run on our left pull me back to the real world. The world where ghosts don't exist.

Nat looks at the dog run. "Too bad you don't have a pet. In a lot of the stories I read, they can see ghosts even when we can't."

"Yeah, I remember that too," I say. "But my mom's allergic to almost all kinds of cats, hamsters, and guinea pigs, and our landlord doesn't allow dogs."

"Not even to visit?" Gus asks. "We could just, you know, bring one by, maybe. . . ."

Nat is not having it. "You can't just bring *any* animal in there. It has to have some connection to the place."

"Who made you the expert?" Gus says. "I say we try it."

I shake my head. "My parents are *not* going to let a dog or cat in our apartment. And definitely not in that room. It has to be perfect for our guests."

"Whatever," Gus grumbles. "You're the one who has to live with the ghost."

We've arrived at my place. I turn to go in. "Thanks, guys. I'll, um, let you know if anything happens."

Gus shoots me a look. "That is, if you make it through the night."

I try not to show how much this freaks me out but clearly fail. Gus bursts out laughing.

"Dude! You should see the look on your face! I'm kidding!"

Nat smacks him on the arm. "That wasn't funny at all. Danny, don't these . . . things . . . normally happen when there are guests?"

I think for a minute. "Yeah . . . for the most part. Like they're disturbing her, or something . . ."

"So you've got nothing to worry about," Nat says.

"At least for tonight!" Gus adds helpfully.

I wave goodbye and head inside.

At dinner, I tell my parents about visiting Katia and show them a copy of the picture Katia printed out with the girl's face.

My mom says, "Danny, I'm sure there's a logical explanation."

My dad wipes his mouth with one of the paper towels we use as napkins when we *don't* have guests. "Film is something I know a little bit about."

This is what he says when he's about to give me a lecture on something he thinks he's an expert on. Okay, he is a filmmaker, but still . . .

"Digital artifacts can look like anything, especially when you zoom in that close," he begins. "I'm not saying you don't see something, just that—"

"Are you telling me you don't see it?"

"See *what*?" he asks. "You say it looks like a girl? People are very suggestible. If I told you it looked like a rabbit, you would probably see a rabbit."

"It doesn't *look like* a girl, it *is* a girl," I say.

My mom pushes my hair back from my forehead. She looks concerned. "I don't think you're getting enough sleep. Kids your age need at least ten hours."

"Tell that to the people coming into my room and waking me up," I mutter.

"Your mom's right," Dad says. "How about an early night?"

"Fine!" I say a little too loudly, pushing my chair back. "How about I take my shower now?"

I stomp off to my room and get clean clothes. I head into

the bathroom, and turn on the water. Part of me doesn't want to take a hot shower so there won't be any steam, but another part (okay, most parts) is *not* about to take a cold shower. I also have my phone with me, so if there *is* another message from our (not so) friendly ghost, I'll have proof this time.

Thankfully, when I peer out of the shower, there's nothing but steam on the mirror.

Maybe I will be left alone tonight.

I get into bed, and there's a soft knock on the door. I stiffen, but it's just my dad. He lowers his head to fit into my room and sits on the corner of my bed.

"I'm sorry about dinner. You feeling any better?"

I nod. "Yeah. I'm sorry too. I know ghosts aren't real. At least, that's what I always thought. But there have been so many—"

"*Changes.* I think that might have something to do with it," my dad says. "You know you don't do well with change."

I want to say I would have been absolutely fine with changing my room to Jake's the way we had originally planned, but decide now is not the time to bring it up. You know what change I'd do really well with? If my parents would stop telling me I don't do well with change.

Dad kisses me on the forehead and looks into my eyes. "I promise, Danny, this is just temporary. I had lunch with Jack Tempkin again, and he says he's got some people in Toronto who are looking for scripts. . . ."

I used to get excited when Dad said things like that. Now I just pretend to be excited. "That's great, Dad. Fingers crossed."

"Right," he says, looking like maybe he's pretending a little too. "Fingers crossed."

He leaves. I drift off to sleep.

When I wake up, I see light under my door. It feels like I've been asleep for ages. I hope I haven't overslept.

I open the door and it's all wrong. The light isn't coming from the windows. It's not sunlight. There's a light glowing in the kitchen.

I try to catch my breath when I see two people sitting at our kitchen table. But it's not our kitchen table. It looks older.

I don't want to join them, but something is pushing me toward the kitchen. As I walk I hear whispers coming from the walls. "Yean . . . ki . . . la . . ." The whispers are all around me as I approach the table.

There is a candle burning in the middle of the table, and plates and glasses, like it's set for a meal or something. One chair is empty.

I realize that the man is my father, with his head down. But he's in clothes from another time. A collarless shirt and old baggy pants.

He gestures for me to join him at the table. As I get closer, I see in the middle of the plate in front of each seat is something small, wrinkled, and black. It looks like a dried brain.

The voices whispering from the walls have changed. Now they're humming a song. The song! *What is that song?*

My mom turns and looks at me, and my dad does the same.

My mother has her hair in a braid and is wearing a lace collar.

There are dark circles under her eyes.

But she has no eyes.

Neither does my father. Sitting in the sockets are what look like almonds, and they're staring at me.

I am shaking so violently now that my mother reaches out.

I think she is doing this to calm me.

But instead, in a girlish voice so different from her own, she screams.

"Where is my little boy?"

CHAPTER 37

THE HUMMING BUBBE

"I guess I fainted. I mean, I've never fainted, but that's what must have happened, because the next thing I remember is my parents shaking me."

Nat is staring at me, her big dark eyes unblinking. "Why were they shaking you?"

"They found me in the kitchen in the morning. I was sitting in a chair, slumped over."

Gus pushes his tray away, his lunch half-eaten. This is a first. "Dude, that is freakier than any ghost story I've ever heard."

Normally Nat would be at chess club during lunch on Friday, but when she got my text, she canceled so she could hear what I had to say.

"So they were eating miniature brains?" Gus asks, eyeing

what's left of his casserole with a queasy look. He pushes it away.

I look down at my own tray, which is hardly touched. I don't have much of an appetite either. "I didn't say there *were* brains. They were something small and wrinkled. It was hard to see in the candlelight."

"So what did your parents do when you told them?" Nat asks.

"They think I should see a therapist."

Gus eats a forkful of noodles, chewing thoughtfully. That didn't last long. "So they think you're nuts?"

"They didn't put it that way," I say carefully. "More like they are *concerned.*"

"So they think you're cracking up," Gus says.

Nat has been folding her napkin into smaller and smaller squares. I've seen her do this with notebook paper when she's trying to work out a particularly difficult math problem. It helps her concentrate.

Finally, she looks up at me. "I don't think you're nuts."

"Gee, thanks," I say.

"Too many weird things have been happening. So what we have to figure out is, if it *is* the girl in the window, who is she?"

Gus scratches his head with his fork. Yes, the same fork he has been eating with. Because Gus. "Is there a ghost directory?"

"Ha ha," says Nat, meaning "not ha ha." "She has to have some connection with the apartment, don't you think?"

"Sure," I answer. "But she could be anyone. I mean, just by looking at her I'd guess she was Eastern European, but I don't know."

"Yeah, but she could also be Italian, Greek, even Arab," suggests Nat, ticking off the possibilities on her fingers. "But at least we can narrow down a little when she was alive."

Gus gives her a skeptical look. "How do you figure?"

"Simple," Nat answers. "Do you know what year the building was built?"

"I dunno," I say. "Sometime around the turn of the century, I guess."

"Well, that's a start," Nat says, gathering her books as the bell rings. "I'm working at the store on Saturday, if you want to come by."

We agree to meet then, since it's the last Friday of the month and Gus and Nat know I have plans.

•← ← ← ←3→

Ever since I can remember, my family has spent at least one Friday a month celebrating Shabbos with my mom's mother, Bubbe Ruth. And yes, when I was little I used to call her "Baby Ruth" and thought the candy bar was named after her,

197

which is a story my mother will be telling people for as long as she lives.

"Bubbe" is Yiddish for "grandmother," and Bubbe Ruth is about as Brooklyn Jewish as they come. I don't mean religious, just the way she talks and acts. For example, most Jews today call the Friday Sabbath meal "Shabbat." But old-school Jews in Brooklyn still say "Good Shabbos" and "Shabbos dinner." When I asked why, Bubbe Ruth said, "When I was a girl, we called it Shabbos. Now everyone wants to be fancy and call it *Shabbat* like they're Sephardic or something."

Apparently Jews like us who came from Russia and Poland used to call it Shabbos, but the Jews from Spain and France and other places call it Shabbat.

I think this is one reason my dad and mom aren't very religious.

It's too complicated.

Don't get me wrong, my parents are proud of being Jewish; they just don't go to services or anything.

But Bubbe Ruth does, at least on the High Holidays. Other than that, my family goes to her place once a month and does all these things like blessing the wine and the braided loaves of challah. My aunt Tracy in Westchester comes with her family when she can, and my uncle Artie brings his family in from California for Thanksgiving.

Bubbe Ruth lives in an old high-rise apartment building farther out in Brooklyn, on Kings Highway, where my mom was brought up. It's nice. My grandfather died a long time ago. But she's not lonely. She has lots of friends.

Well, neighbors, anyway.

Who we hear all about.

Especially right after they leave the elevator.

"*Her* I can't stand" is a typical Bubbe Ruth comment.

When we arrive at her building it's already pretty close to sundown. According to Jewish law, we're supposed to be inside and celebrating by now, but we're kind of loose about that. We have to change trains to get to Bubbe Ruth's, so it usually takes longer than if we had a car. Brooklyn is a lot bigger than you might think.

I press the button with GERSON 16E printed next to it.

There is a long pause, and then the intercom crackles. It's hard to hear through all the static.

"Who is it?" Bubbe Ruth yells. All these years and Mom has yet to convince her that she doesn't have to speak quite so loudly into the microphone.

"It's us!" I yell back.

"Who?"

My mother pushes me out of the way. "Mom! Let us in!"

After a few more questions, Bubbe Ruth finally accepts that it is indeed her family and we're buzzed in. Immediately I'm hit with the same smells as always—a combination of cabbage, chicken, and pickles. I'm guessing that's what it is, because to be honest, it's just "old people apartment" smells to me.

We take the elevator, which is working (not a given). As soon as the door opens we hear Bubbe Ruth's booming voice. "Hello! Hello! What happened? The subway was broken?"

"The subway wasn't broken," my mom says, kissing her.

"It's just that you're so late," Bubbe Ruth murmurs.

My dad hands her a bag of rugelach from Haddad's. "We're fifteen minutes late."

She ignores his comment and admires the pastries. "You brought! From the Arab place, right?"

We've been bringing her rugelach from Haddad's for as long as I can remember, and she still calls it "the Arab place." Old people . . . they don't always say things in the nicest way.

Bubbe Ruth looks at me, and a huge smile creases her wide face. I see a little of Mom in her when she smiles. "Danele! Such a big boy he is!"

DAN-ah-luh. That's Bubbe's way of saying Danny.

She then adds something that sounds like "kenna hora poo poo poo."

I remember asking my mom why she does this, and my mom shrugged and said she *always* says it after saying something good. I looked it up and it's actually spelled *kein ayin hara,* which is Yiddish for "May the evil eye stay away," and the "poo poo poo" part is when you spit three times between your fingers to help ward off the evil eye. It's kind of like knocking on wood. I guess so many bad things have happened to the Jews throughout history that when you say something nice you have to say this right after to make sure it won't bring on some sort of misery.

Bubbe Ruth sighs. You have never heard a real sigh until you've heard my Bubbe sigh. It's like her whole body is sighing. It's like she's sighing for all the grandmothers everywhere on the planet.

"It's wonderful Jakele is off to his college—such a brilliant boy! But I miss having him here."

"We all miss him," Mom tells her.

Bubbe Ruth sighs again.

We all stand there missing Jake, and then Bubbe Ruth springs into action.

"Okay, enough about Jake. The food will overcook."

Bubbe Ruth hustles us into her dining room, which is already set with nice china. I can smell chicken for real this time.

She and my mother light the candles and say the blessing, and my dad and I say, "Omayn," which is the Jewish way of saying "amen."

Bubbe Ruth heads to the kitchen, humming away. She is, as my uncle Artie likes to point out, *always* humming. It drives him crazy. "Stop humming, Ma!" he'll yell.

Bubbe Ruth just waves her hand. "Who is it hurting?"

I kind of like her humming. I mean, it's never an actual song, just some notes going up and down occasionally. But Uncle Artie can't stand it.

"Ma, at least hum a song!" he'll yell.

Bubbe Ruth laughs. "I am."

"You could have fooled me," Uncle Artie mutters.

As I say, it's always been just random notes.

Until tonight.

Tonight the notes sound familiar.

A chill goes through my body.

I am finding it hard to breathe normally, because this feels like the ghost has reached all the way from our house to my bubbe's warm apartment.

I try to sound casual when I ask, "Bubbe, what's that song you're humming?"

She laughs like always. "Tonight he asks? It's what I always hum. I used to sing it to your mother when she was a baby, remember, darling? And I sang it to you too. It's a Yiddish lullaby."

I need to know. "What's it called?"

She thinks for a minute. Hums a few bars of the song I've come to know so well, and to dread.

Her face lights up. "'*Rozhinkes mit mandlen*,'" she announces.

I am back in my dream, at that kitchen table. That horrible, terrible kitchen table of my worst nightmare. So I ask, "What does that mean in English?"

"'Raisins and Almonds,' of course," Bubbe Ruth says.

CHAPTER 38

THE POSSESSION OF MRS. NAOMI FELDSTEIN

I glare at Mom. "I hummed that tune to you a dozen times! You didn't remember it?"

Mom looks annoyed. "It didn't sound like that when you hummed it."

Bubbe Ruth looks at my mom with amusement. "*Nu,* your son doesn't seem to mind my humming."

"It's just that I've heard that same song being hummed in our apartment for the past few weeks, and I couldn't figure out what it was," I say.

"You know, Danny, she hummed it when you were a baby, too," my dad grumbles, defending my mom. "Why didn't *you* remember it?"

I flop down onto one of Bubbe Ruth's chairs, which is

filled with old *People* magazines. "When I was a *baby*! Who remembers things from when they were a baby?"

"Maybe you do, without realizing it," my mom says softly.

That stops me cold. What if I'm just hearing the tune in my head? What if it's something I happened to remember for no reason? What if there's no ghostly singing?

Bubbe Ruth has had enough. "Will someone please tell me what's going on? Mamele, darling, turn off the stove."

She calls my mother Mamele (pronounced MAM-uh-luh) even though my mom is her daughter. Then again, she calls the Caribbean woman who delivers the mail Mamele too. She even calls my cousin Lila, who is just eighteen and going to college, Mamele. I guess that's what old Jewish ladies call everyone.

So I tell her. I tell her everything. From the knocking on the door to the strange girl in the window to Mrs. Sarah Delano Cabot. And finally the nightmare of the kitchen table.

I assume Bubbe Ruth will laugh and pat my hand, like she usually does when I tell her anything, but instead she listens intently, leaning forward and staring at me through her thick glasses. Every once in a while, a small "oy" escapes her lips.

When I'm finished, she leans back in her chair and sighs. Maybe I'm wrong. Maybe all grandmothers sigh like this. But I have a feeling Mrs. Sarah Delano Cabot's mother does not sigh like this.

She doesn't say anything for a long time as she sits there,

my mother fussing in the kitchen, preparing the food. This is also something that has never happened. For Bubbe Ruth not to supervise my mother is breaking a tradition as old as I can remember. Her face looks like all the blood has drained out of it.

My dad is concerned. "Ruth, are you all right? Should I call a doctor?"

Bubbe Ruth waves her hand. "A doctor I don't need. A rabbi, maybe."

My mom rushes over. "Mom, you're . . . not dying or anything?" she asks, which is a pretty funny way to find out how someone is feeling if you ask me, but Bubbe Ruth just looks annoyed.

"Of course I'm not dying, Mamele. Danele here is the one who needs the rabbi."

Bubbe Ruth peers at me, then cocks her head. "Go touch the mezuzah."

Okay, if you're not Jewish, that is going to sound *really* weird. A mezuzah is a wooden or silver box containing some biblical verses that's attached to the doorpost of a Jewish home.

Even though she's not particularly religious, Bubbe Ruth has one on her door, and my dad and mom always touch it on the way in. For good luck, I guess. Or out of respect.

Like saying *kein ayin hara,* a mezuzah is supposed to keep evil away from the house. Jews have a lot of things they do to keep evil away. It seems to me those things haven't helped them too much in the last two thousand years, but whenever I say that, my dad says, "Don't be smart."

I look at Bubbe Ruth funny. Why should I go out and touch the mezuzah?

She's getting annoyed. "Your ears stopped working? Touch the mezuzah."

I shrug and get up and go to the front door. I reach up and touch the mezuzah. "There, I've done it. Happy now?"

Bubbe Ruth looks relieved. "That's good, darling. It means you're not the one who is possessed. If the evil spirit was in you, you wouldn't be able to do that."

My dad takes off his glasses and rubs his hands through his hair. "Please don't encourage him," he says evenly.

Bubbe Ruth looks at him. "Who's encouraging? I'm just telling him what he needs to know."

My mother has put the food on the table. "Come eat!" she calls.

We sit down, and after Bubbe Ruth blesses the challah loaf, we start to eat.

"What did you mean, 'what he needs to know'?" I ask.

Bubbe Ruth holds up her fork. "Talking later. First we eat."

Finally, after all the dishes are washed and put away, and we've had "a little cake" and some of the rugelach from

Haddad's, and I'm jumping out of my skin I'm so impatient, Bubbe eases herself into her old recliner.

Rubbing her hands, she nods.

"So! I'm no expert, but it sounds like you have gotten yourself a dybbuk," she announces.

"Oh, Mom," my mother says. "Please don't do this."

Bubbe Ruth gives her daughter a sharp look. "Listen to Miss Know-It-All. Well, you *don't* know it all, Mamele. If he's hearing someone singing 'Raisins and Almonds,' it's a Jewish ghost."

"We're not living in the shtetl, Ruth," my dad says, referring to the little villages in Russia where Jews used to live, like in *Fiddler on the Roof.* "This is Brooklyn."

Bubbe Ruth doesn't even look at him. "You think there aren't dybbuks in Brooklyn? Ask your aunt Sheila."

My mother sighs. "Aunt Sheila has been dead for five years."

"Sheila, may she rest in peace, always talked about her neighbor. You never heard?"

My dad closes his eyes. He clearly wants this conversation to end, but he knows that's not going to happen anytime soon. "I remember Sheila saying something, but—"

"Her neighbor Naomi Feldstein, she was possessed by the spirit of her husband's first wife. A terrible business."

"You mean that's what she told him when she went out

and spent a fortune on a new living room set and put it on their credit card," Mom says.

"Go ahead and laugh. That wasn't the only thing," Bubbe Ruth replies.

Dad turns to me and whispers, "She had a little fling with her periodontist."

Bubbe Ruth whirls toward him. "I heard that! It wasn't her fault. She had the dybbuk in her!"

"So I have a few questions," I say.

My dad nods. "Okay, a periodontist is a special kind of dentist who takes care of your gums."

"No!" I say. "What is this dybbuk, anyway?"

Bubbe Ruth takes my hand. "Darling, don't be scared." Which is what people say when they expect you to be scared out of your wits.

"A dybbuk is a restless spirit," she says. "A dead person who can't move on to the next life. Someone in your apartment has unfinished business. Sometimes a dybbuk is there to torment you. But sometimes it's there because it needs help. I think this one needs you."

CHAPTER 39

DYBBUK OR IBBUR?

My father groans. "This is *literally* a *bubbe meise.*"

"That's Yiddish for 'old wives' tale,'" my mother explains.

I should say this is the most Yiddish I have ever heard any-one outside of Bubbe Ruth use in my family.

Bubbe Ruth tugs at my sleeve. "Listen, Danele, I don't want to frighten you. It might *not* be a dybbuk."

My mom looks relieved. "Thank you, Mom. Listen to your grandmother, Danny."

"It could be an *ibbur.* That's a nicer spirit. They don't wish you harm."

The sound of my dad face-palming could be heard in the next apartment, I bet.

"Ruth, you're not helping," he says.

She glares at him. "*I'm* not helping? You let your son be scared out of his mind by a restless spirit, and I'm the one who's not helping?" She turns to me. "So as I was saying, a dybbuk is usually hanging around for two reasons. One, there is some unfinished business. Something left behind, or disturbed. Or else it is there to torment a guilty person, someone who did a bad thing."

Bubbe Ruth looks me in the eye. "Did you do a bad thing?"

I think hard. I mean, I'm not perfect, but I haven't killed anyone. Or stolen anything.

"Not that I can think of. I guess I told my parents I was doing my homework a few times when I was actually playing video games."

Bubbe Ruth laughs. "For that, you don't get haunted. It could also be an *ibbur.* That's a righteous person who stays behind to guide the living to a virtuous life or to help them accomplish something."

"But why our apartment? And why now?" I ask.

Bubbe Ruth side-eyes my dad. "All I can tell you is that a dybbuk cannot enter a house with a mezuzah. I told your father to put one up when you moved in, but no, he knew better."

"Not this again," my dad groans.

Bubbe Ruth shrugs. "I'm just saying."

"She doesn't seem very happy," I say.

Bubbe Ruth nods. "You know it's a she, which is a good first step."

"First step in what?" my mother asks.

Bubbe Ruth looks at her daughter like she's an idiot. "The first step in getting rid of her, of course."

"Wait. You know how to get rid of the dybbuk?" I ask excitedly.

"We don't know if it's a dybbuk," chides Bubbe Ruth. "But yes."

My father has had enough. "Enough already. You're just making things worse."

Bubbe Ruth's voice is getting louder. "I'm making things worse? If you'd told me about this when things started—"

My mom steps in. "Okay, let's just calm down. No yelling."

"Who's yelling?" yells Bubbe Ruth. "I'm just talking regular."

"Mom!"

Bubbe Ruth speaks in a very loud whisper. "Is this better?"

Dad sighs. "Just talk like you normally do."

Bubbe Ruth smiles and rubs her hands. "Fine. Lovely. So let's assume this is a dybbuk. To get rid of a dybbuk, we have to find out why it hasn't moved on. You have to interview it."

"I have to do what?"

"This is how you get the information you need to convince it to leave. And very important: You need to learn its name. Or what it was called when it was in our world."

"What does that do?" I ask.

"Knowing the name allows you to command it," she declares.

My dad has kept quiet as long as he can. "According to who?"

"People who know about these things, that's who," Bubbe Ruth says simply.

"Like you?" Dad says, barely keeping it together.

Bubbe turns and looks at him. "I'll have you know, Mr. I Don't Go to Services or Put a Mezuzah on My Front Door, that in the old country, my grandfather Mordechai, may he rest in peace, helped rid many of his neighbors of dybbuks. He was known all over Kiev. He told me stories. I remember."

My dad turns and whispers to my mom. "She barely remembers what she had for lunch, but she remembers this."

"I heard that!" Bubbe Ruth shouts. For an old lady, she hears pretty well.

I hug her. "Thanks for all the good information, Bubbe. I promise if this spirit shows up again, I will try to get her to talk to me."

Bubbe Ruth seems delighted by my hug. I hear her saying softly—well, softly for her—to my parents, "Listen. If it helps him get a good night's sleep, isn't it worth it?"

I let go of Bubbe, and my dad has a totally different expression on his face. He hugs Bubbe Ruth too, and thanks her.

"I'm sorry. You know something? You are a very wise lady," he says.

Bubbe Ruth laughs and hits him on the shoulder, and then I swear she winks at my mother. "Enough foolishness. It's getting late!"

CHAPTER 40

ASAKO AND TOMOKO

"So that's it. Either I'm full-on crazy, or there's some Jewish spirit who needs my help to right some wrong or find relief from her torment."

I've just finished catching up Nat and Gus on all that's happened and all that I've learned since I last saw them.

Nat is silent, turning over everything I've said in her mind.

There is an unmistakable crunching sound from Gus. It's clear from the bulge in his cheek that, yet again, he has put an entire ultimate malted milk ball in his mouth.

"Hey! Where'd you get that?" Nat snaps. "You better not have taken it from the jar without asking."

Gus holds up a plastic bag with a dozen more malted milk balls in it, with a price label affixed to it, showing that he actually bought them. "My allowance."

He crunches again.

"Do you have to do that?" Nat asks.

Gus smiles, trying to swallow what's in his mouth. "Helf me fink."

"You're drooling again," I point out.

Gus wipes his mouth with his sleeve.

"We have like a thousand napkins in this store, Gus. That's so gross," Nat growls.

Typically at this point Gus would answer by seeing how many malted milk balls he could fit in his mouth at one time just to see Nat's reaction, but we are interrupted.

"Gus Baublitz has decided to become a customer? This is my lucky day!" It's Sammy, beaming even more than usual, his voice filling the store. Haddad's has just opened, so customers won't be filling up the store for a few more minutes. Sammy has time to chat.

He reaches behind Nat and rearranges the gourmet mustards on the shelf. As he works he talks to us. "How's the meat business treating your father?" he asks Gus.

"He's good," Gus says.

Sammy smiles. "It's hard to find a good butcher, you know. It's *rare* to get the job *well done.*"

He never tires of telling corny jokes, but it feels good, because it's so normal. He turns to me.

"How's your ghost problem?"

I tell him a little bit about Bubbe Ruth.

He nods. "A lovely lady, your grandmother. I haven't seen her in ages. She should come by the store."

"She doesn't get down here all that often," I say. "It's hard for her to use the subway, and—"

Sammy waves a hand in annoyance. "She doesn't need the subway. The city has free senior vans that'll take her anywhere she wants to go."

"I'm not sure she wants to go anywhere," I admit.

Sammy looks stern. He folds his arms. "You tell her I'm very hurt she hasn't come to visit the store. I'll even have one of the ladies make her cabbage soup."

"I'll give her the message," I promise.

From the other side of the store, like always, an excited voice calls out, "Sammy!" As if someone's seeing a long-lost relative. This time it's an Asian woman with her husband and two uncomfortable kids who look like they're our age.

Sammy looks at us and grins. "It's showtime!" He turns and says, "Eleanor!"

She beams because he's remembered her name. This scene is going to be repeated dozens of times today, but to her it's special.

Eleanor pushes her kids forward. "You remember Stephen and Laura?"

"Of course!" Sammy exclaims. "They've gotten so big!"

I wonder how many times he's said that over the past thirty years.

I turn to see Nat still lost in thought. Finally, she says, "I'm glad you found out what the song is."

"Do you think I'm just remembering it from when I was a baby?" I ask.

Nat shakes her head. "I think whatever happened isn't about you. It's about that girl in the window. She's some poor soul worried about her little boy."

"She looked a little young to be a mother," Gus says.

Nat nods. "But girls had babies a lot younger then."

"We don't know when 'then' is," I remind her. "I mean, it could be any time. And it doesn't have to be a baby. It could be her little brother. Or a doll. Who knows?"

"That's true," Nat says. "So how are we going to find out?"

Gus reaches into his bag for another ultimate malted milk ball. "I guess you'll have to ask her, huh?"

＊＜＜＜＜３＋

My parents and I have finished dinner, and there's a sense of anticipation as we wait for Asako and Tomoko to return from their Broadway show. Well, anticipation from my parents. And dread from me. Who knows what tonight might bring?

They arrived this morning and dropped off their bags. According to their application, they're both twenty-five and "office workers," whatever that is.

Mom has watched a bunch of videos online because she

wants to be nice to them. She bows when they come in, which makes my dad crazy because he thinks she's being ridiculous. We're not Japanese. The closest thing is my aunt Amanda's family—they're Japanese American, which of course my mom wants to tell Asako and Tomoko. As if they care.

They bow back and smile.

"Our room is where, please?" asks Asako, the taller one. They both have long straight hair. Asako's is light brown. She seems comfortable trying out her English. Tomoko is more reserved and tends to look at the floor a lot. I bet I'd be that way if I ever visited Japan.

My mom takes them to the room, chattering away about her sister-in-law and how the family came over from Japan to Hawaii, and have they ever been to Hawaii?

My dad is glued to his monitor. His jaw is tight, and his mouth a straight line. He hates the idea that Mom is patronizing them. He said to her, "I'm begging you. Just be polite. They might be shy."

My mom was annoyed. "I just want them to feel *welcome*."

It turns out Asako and Tomoko already have a list of things they want to get done while they're here. Tomoko has a notebook with a picture of a fried egg with a face on the cover. It's very cute, which even I know the Japanese word for, *kawaii*. I know it because so many kids at school are into Japanese pop culture. They watch a lot of anime. A *lot*. It's a good thing Gus isn't here or he'd ask them all about some show he's watched a hundred episodes of, and who knows if they even are into that stuff?

As soon as Asako and Tomoko dropped off their bags and freshened up, they ran out, because they wanted to have breakfast at Junior's, which is a Brooklyn landmark, world famous for its cheesecake.

They have things printed out from the Internet, from a Japanese website that is clearly about all the things you have to do in Brooklyn. I am blown away to see that one of them is visiting Haddad's!

There's a buzz at the door, and my mom springs up. Asako and Tomoko are there, festooned with shopping bags from various shops and souvenir places. They are each clutching a Playbill from some Broadway musical I've never heard of. They seem very happy and excited. My mother bows again, and then catching my dad's glare she apologizes, which sets off another round of giggles from the two women. I don't think it's because they think it's funny, they're just uncomfortable.

Tomoko shyly asks Asako something in Japanese. Asako turns to me. "Is all right for to use the bathroom?"

"No problem!" I say.

Asako looks confused. "It's a problem?"

"No!" I assure her. "It is *not* a problem. It is okay. Just let me know when you're finished."

"Ah, yes, okay," she says, giving me a small bow.

The bathroom schedule is clearly the worst part of this whole experience. Nobody wants to share a bathroom with a teenage boy, which is understandable.

It's a lot later when I finally brush my teeth and head to my room. I get into bed and try to fall asleep.

Knowing that something will happen tonight, I brace myself for a knock on the door. Or a visitation. Or anything. I wait, listening to the sound of my shallow breathing. But nothing happens.

I drift off, and it seems as though I might actually get a good night's rest, until I feel someone poking me.

It's Tomoko. But of course it isn't. Her eyes are wide open, unfocused. There is the same glow about her, and her hair is standing straight up on her head. I've prepared myself for this, but it is still terrifying.

I fight the urge to scream, and try to remember Bubbe's Ruth's advice. I need to talk to whoever has taken over the body of Tomoko.

The young girl's voice is coming out of her mouth, asking the same question. "Where is my little boy?"

I'm actually getting annoyed with this ghost, dybbuk or not. From somewhere, I find my voice and say, "Look, I don't know where your little boy is."

She turns and looks me full in the face. It's like she's seeing me for the first time. She looks confused, and angry.

"Who are you?" she demands.

I've had it. "Who am I? I'm Danny Kantrowitz, and I live here. Who are *you*?"

Her eyes widen in fright, and she backs away. "Where is Rochele? What have you done with her?"

Now we're getting somewhere. I'm not sure where, but at least she's asking a different question.

"What's your name?" I ask her.

"Where is Rochele? I want to speak to Rochele!" She is almost screaming. I hear footsteps outside my room.

"What's your name?" I demand.

Her eyes roll to the back of her head, and she drops to the floor.

As my parents open the door I reach out to Tomoko.

She is ice cold.

CHAPTER 41

CLICK HERE TO HELP

Asako is right behind my parents, and she rushes to her friend, who is murmuring something in Japanese. Asako rubs Tomoko's hands and my mother steps in.

She is in full mother mode. These women may be in their twenties and from a totally different culture, but a mom is a mom. She insists on bringing Tomoko to the bathroom to take a hot shower to warm up and then to the kitchen to make her a cup of hot tea.

Both women are bowing and saying, "Thank you, not necessary," over and over, but they know better than to argue.

After about an hour, things settle down, and Tomoko is led back to the room. Asako says that Tomoko is allergic to cats. Had we ever had a cat?

I don't want to point out that that was a heck of an allergic reaction to cat dander.

"No, I'm allergic too. Maybe there was a cat outside, on the fire escape," my mom suggests.

Asako nods. "Yes, perhaps," she says thoughtfully.

My father looks skeptical. "Maureen, the window was closed."

"You don't know," my mother says. "Maybe she's *really allergic*."

She pats Asako's hand. Asako looks uncomfortable. I don't blame her. I try to imagine something like this happening to me in Japan, and I think I'd be a lot less chill about the whole thing.

Everybody seems to want to believe that this was some sort of allergic reaction, and I don't even get into her asking about the boy again, or freaking out when I asked her name. I know my folks will say I was just misunderstanding something she said in Japanese.

Asako says good night and bows. She apologizes yet again, and my mother waves her off. Asako looks totally embarrassed, as if it was her fault.

After she's headed back to the room, I can't help myself. "Isn't it odd that all these people keep coming into my room? I mean, I didn't imagine *that*."

"It's only been two guests," my mother says. "And they were both, well . . . travel is very disorienting."

"We really need to get a sign for the bathroom," my dad adds. "I think late at night it's confusing for people."

My mom nods violently. "Yes! That's a *great* idea, sweetheart." She turns to me. "I'm sure that will stop your night visitors."

I am not going to win this argument. They are both too stubborn to see what's in front of them. I look at the time. One in the morning.

"I need to get back to sleep," I announce.

"We all do," Dad says, and hugs me.

I go back to my room and take out my phone. It occurs to me that we've got a puzzle on our hands here: how to get this dybbuk, or whatever it is, to speak to me.

I realize that there is someone who knows more about solving puzzles than anyone else, and not only does he live in California (where it's only ten p.m.), but he's my cousin.

I text Ted to see if he's awake, knowing full well he's probably playing some computer game or other. Whenever he visits for Thanksgiving with Uncle Artie and Aunt Amanda, he tries to get me to play these escape-the-room video games with him, but they're too hard for me. Ted is amazing at them, though. He even made the news last summer, because he and two friends solved a treasure hunt that Aunt Amanda's uncle had set up before he died. I don't remember too much about it, except that Ted looked kind of goofy on TV, and they mentioned that the girl who helped them went to private school here, Saint Anselm's, before moving to California.

Ted texts back that it's cool to FaceTime. My phone makes the familiar tinkling sound, and I accept his call.

I see Ted smiling at me. "Hey, dude. What's up?"

I try to fill him in on what's happened. He's totally ticked off on my behalf about not getting Jake's room, and it's hard for me to move him past that. But eventually we get around to the real issue.

"Ted, I didn't call to whine about the room," I say.

I tell him all about what's happened, all the weird stuff. He doesn't laugh or tell me I'm nuts. He just nods.

"So . . . you don't think it's all in my head?" I ask.

Ted has a funny expression on his face and he glances at his laptop. "I dunno, man. Before this thing happened last summer, maybe I wouldn't have thought it possible. But there are definitely things that you just can't explain, you know?"

"For sure," I say. I go on to tell him what Bubbe Ruth said.

I notice a small smile appear. "Oh. Bubbe Ruth."

"Look," I say. "I know she's kind of . . . I don't know . . ."

"Nuts?" Ted suggests. He sees that I'm not laughing, and he gets serious. "Okay, let's say she's right. I mean, I know she's hung up on this mezuzah thing. She was thrilled to find out that Lila's roommate at college is Jewish and had already nailed a mezuzah on the doorpost before Lila got there. Bubbe Ruth is convinced that's why Lila is doing so well. So yeah, I dunno. Why not just put up a mezuzah now?"

"It's too late," I tell him. "Once you've got a dybbuk, or whatever it is, she said you have to get rid of it."

Ted thinks for a second. "Okay, you know the ghost is humming a lullaby, and you know she speaks English. What you need to do is find out why she's unhappy. Maybe there was a boy she loved and he died in the war?"

"But then she'd know where he was, right?"

"Or maybe it was someone she wanted to marry but her parents forbid it."

"That's possible," I say. "But how am I going to find out? I tried asking her. She freaked out."

I can see the wheels in Ted's head turning. Like he's playing one of his games with me. "You need to learn her name. That's the most important thing. Get that and I bet you can unlock all the others. Now let's solve the first clue. Who did she ask to speak to?"

"Someone named Rochele," I say.

Ted looks at me the way he does when something is obvious to him but I'm not seeing it. "Think of Bubbe Ruth. She calls you Danele. She calls your mom Mamele. She calls my dad Mr. Smarty-Pants, so that doesn't really count."

"So . . . Rochele . . . Rochel . . ."

"Probably Rachel, don't you think?" Ted says. "So we know she had someone close to her in life named Rachel. A sister . . ."

I smile at him. "Or a cousin. You're amazing."

"Nah," Ted says. "You've still got a lot of work ahead of you. But I bet there are resources right there in Brooklyn. It's such an old place, people must be doing research on buildings all the time. If it was me, I'd try to find out all the people who lived in your apartment who had a sister named Rachel."

Ted checks his phone. "Jeez, Danny, it's almost two in the morning where you are! Get some sleep, dude!"

I yawn. "Yeah, I think I will. And I think I'm going to sleep better than I have in a while."

CHAPTER 42

THE MUSTACHE IS WAXED TODAY

I wake up in the morning to the sound of my parents having a disagreement in the kitchen. I hear my mother say, "She didn't have to do this!"

Then my father answers, for what sounds like not the first time (my mom tends to repeat herself when she's upset), "Maureen, we have to respect her wishes."

I join them and see a note on the table. It's written in perfect cursive on a lined sheet of paper with a little egg-yolk person in one corner. The note reads:

> *Please accept once again our sincere apologies for disturbing everyone last night. We are so sorry, and have chosen to find accommodations elsewhere for the remainder of our trip. We very much enjoyed meeting*

you and hope you will not think badly of us. Thank
you for all your attention and good wishes.

Best,
Tomoko and Asako

My mother gestures at the paper and looks up at me. "Can you believe this? They must have packed up and left in the middle of the night."

She crosses her arms tightly. "I want to refund their money, but your dad insists that would only make them more uncomfortable."

"I just think they're embarrassed," Dad replies. "I know it's silly to us, but I get the feeling that they didn't think they could face us after what happened."

My mom gives me a look. "All of a sudden your father has become an expert on Japanese culture."

I get some cereal out of the cupboard and pour myself a bowl. "They were probably scared. I can definitely understand if they didn't want a repeat performance of last night."

I know *I* don't.

My mom sits down next to me and hands me a napkin. "That's ridiculous. She just was out of sorts from the flight. It's a long flight, after all."

I wasn't going to get into the fact that most people with jet lag don't rush into some poor kid's room and act like a long-dead girl asking about her little boy. That boat has sailed. Or that plane has left. Or—okay, you get the idea.

I let my parents figure out which of them knows more about the proper way to engage with young Japanese women (spoiler alert: neither of them) and change and head off to school.

I get there early and Nat is already there, eager to hear what happened. I tell her about my conversation with Ted.

"What a help," she says.

"I know, right?" I answer.

Nat rolls her eyes. "I was being sarcastic. I could have figured that out. That's the easy part. Duh. We need to find out who Rachel is. And what her relationship to the dybbuk is."

Gus walks up at the tail end of the conversation. "She could be a friendly ghost."

"She sure doesn't seem friendly," Nat says. "She seems totally mad."

It seems so weird to discuss this in the school hallway, on what feels like just another totally normal day. Like something like this can't really be happening. The noise around us, the babble of voices and giggles and general rushing off to class, this is real life. And yet . . .

Finally, I look up. "I don't think she's mad. I think she's upset. And sad. She needs to hear that her little boy is okay, for some reason."

"But first we need to learn who she is, right?" asks Gus.

"Yeah," I admit. "And I haven't a clue as to how we're going to do that."

Nat gets an "aha!" look on her face. "I know who would know all about it."

She turns and heads briskly toward the staircase, and Gus and I rush to catch up with her.

As soon as Nat stops on the third floor and turns right, toward the teachers' lounge, I have a feeling I know who she's thinking of.

She knocks on the door and peers in. Her face lights up. "Mr. Nordstrom! Do you have a few minutes before your next class?"

Mr. Nordstrom is in the middle of taking a bite of pastry, but he gestures with his free hand for us to come in. By the time I've closed the door, he's washed down his Danish with a swig from his water bottle. He is dressed, as usual, in his own style, which is hard to describe.

Mr. Nordstrom is not an old guy, but he dresses like an old professor from the movies or something. He always wears things like tweed jackets and fancy leather shoes with red soles and white shoelaces. Today he's in a mustard-yellow cardigan sweater with leather patches on the elbows, and a bow tie. Of course he has a beard; sometimes (like today) he even waxes the ends of his mustache.

I guess you could say he is a *character*. But he's also an awesome teacher, and really easy to talk to.

"And a very good morning to you, students!" he exclaims. He tends to exclaim everything he says. "How may I be of assistance?"

"I'm . . . doing research for a project," I say. "It's about the house I live in. I'm trying to find out all the people who've lived there."

Mr. Nordstrom's face lights up. He rubs his hands together. "What a *great* idea! The houses in Brooklyn have such stories to tell!"

"Especially this one," Gus says. "It has a— Ow!"

Nat has bumped into him. Hard. "Oops. Sorry, Gus. Yes, it has a long history."

Gus glares at Nat and checks his ribs. "That's going to leave a bruise."

Nat ignores him. "I told Danny if anyone knew where he could find that information, it would be you."

Mr. Nordstrom smiles. "I really should make you figure this out for yourself. There is the Internet, you know. Or . . ." He pauses, like in class.

"We could try the library," I suggest. "But I wouldn't know where to look for something this specific."

"If only there was a place that was dedicated to learning all about the history of Brooklyn," Gus says wistfully.

Mr. Nordstrom looks almost giddy. "You mean . . . like a *historical society?*"

Nat laughs, while Gus and I look on in confusion. "You

guys," Nat says, "don't you remember when we had a field trip last year for our research papers for Mr. Nordstrom's class?"

It's kind of embarrassing that we didn't think of the Brooklyn Historical Society before. If there's any place that has the answers we need, that would be it.

CHAPTER 43

A HISTORICAL TRIP

I do remember the trip to the Brooklyn Historical Society, which was cool because it's right here in Brooklyn Heights, on one of the older streets.

The historical society is as grand and imposing as I remembered. The building has all this stuff carved into the stones outside, and when our class visited, Mr. Nordstrom pointed them out: the busts of famous people like Benjamin Franklin, Christopher Columbus, William Shakespeare, and Ludwig van Beethoven, and also ones of an American Indian and a Viking right over the entrance, representing the first people here in Brooklyn.

Nat raised her hand and said, "I notice they're all men, and all are white, except for the Indian, and his land was taken away from him." Mr. Nordstrom looked really happy that Nat had said this, and nodded. I felt bad because I hadn't noticed it until Nat said something.

To get to the library, you have to take this big dark wood staircase with soft lighting, so you feel like you're stepping back in time, especially as you climb the stairs and see these huge oil paintings of guys who a lot of the streets in the Heights are named after. "More white guys," Nat had said with a sniff.

Somehow it's a lot more intimidating to go through those huge doors and into that hushed hallway all by ourselves, without the other kids and a teacher. Our steps echo as we walk up the stairs, which I hadn't noticed last year, when everyone was chattering and pushing each other.

We walk into the Othmer Library (that's what's written on the door) and approach the main desk, which is raised above the reading area. There are about a half a dozen people doing research, with their laptops open to take notes.

And there's plenty to do research on. During our field trip, the librarian showed us a record of a slave auction in 1786, and the bill of sale of a house from the 1860s and even a Brooklyn Dodgers uniform, along with the newspaper from 1955 when Brooklyn won the World Series. I bet the Old Man would have loved to see that.

The library looks exactly like the library in the Harry Potter movies, with lamps hanging from a high, high ceiling, and row after row of bookcases. But in this case, the books weren't about magic, just history. I guess if they could help us learn the name of my dybbuk, they would be pretty magical too.

As we get to the main desk, a young lady with big glasses and her hair pulled back walks briskly over and regards us. She has sort of a severe expression on her face, the kind I think librarians have to practice. Or maybe they're just born that way.

School librarians are always smiling. Well, unless the students are horsing around, and then they can lose it. Which is understandable. But it takes a lot to get them mad.

Anyway, this librarian doesn't look like she's in a bad mood, just like she's all business. "Hello, children," she says. "Are you meeting with a school group?"

Nat is best at talking to people, so Gus and I look to her. "No, we're here to do some research for a term paper," she says, smiling her nicest smile. There is a sign on the desk that says MS. DYER, HEAD LIBRARIAN, so Nat takes a chance. "And we could use some help finding things?"

Bingo! Ms. Dyer's expression changes, and she smiles back. When she smiles, her whole face lights up. It's pretty clear that she senses a kindred spirit, the way Gus does when he meets someone else who loves anime.

"What exactly are you researching?" Ms. Dyer asks.

Nat turns to me, so I unglue my lips. "Um, I live in one of the buildings on Willow Street, and I thought it would be cool to write about all the people who lived there."

Ms. Dyer nods. "What a great idea! Well, we have *lots* of resources for that!"

She gestures for us to follow her. Nat reaches into her backpack for a pen and paper.

"Oh, you'll have to leave that here in a cubby," Ms. Dyer says, and takes Nat's bag. "And no pens. Only pencils allowed in this library."

"You don't want kids writing in the books, huh?" Gus asks.

Ms. Dyer gives him one of her smiles and says, "Well, yes, that's the idea. But it's not just kids, it's everyone." She leans in and cocks her head toward all the grown-ups at the tables doing their work. "You'd be surprised who are the worst culprits."

Nat takes a pencil from the desk, and we walk past the tables to one of the shelves. Ms. Dyer indicates a wall of books covered in blue fabric. "These go back to the 1860s and list everyone who lived in Brooklyn. You'd have to go through them year by year."

There are at least a hundred of them. It would take weeks, I think.

Ms. Dyer's expression changes. "But these are only the society people, the ones people thought were important."

"The person we're looking for isn't all that important, probably," Nat says. I think of the girl's lace collar, but I guess Nat doesn't want to look through all those books either.

Ms. Dyer thinks for a minute and then takes us to another part of the library, where there are computers. "Here might be a good place to start." She sits in front of one and types something, and a website pops up. "This is a wonderful resource," she says. "It's scans of the *Brooklyn Daily Eagle,* the entire newspaper, going back to its first issues. If you type in an address, it will show you all the times any person who lived there was ever mentioned in the paper."

This sounds a whole lot easier than looking at hundreds of books.

There is a hushed call across the library, and we see another librarian waving at Ms. Dyer, holding a phone.

Ms. Dyer waves, then turns back to us and takes Nat's pencil and writes something on her pad. "I have to take this call. But if you do find a name, you can go to this ancestry site and put the name in and any census form or document will show you who else might have been living there as well."

"That's *awesome*!" Gus says a little too loudly. He and libraries are not a natural fit. He is so used to people glaring at him, he doesn't even notice all the glares from the research tables. Ms. Dyer wishes us good luck and rushes off to answer the phone.

We turn to the keyboard, and I type "42 Willow Street." To my surprise, dozens of entries pop up.

I click on the first one, and a page of an old newspaper fills the screen. It's packed with type, from top to bottom. Not like today's papers. This was the only way for people to get their news, so I guess newspapers crammed as much as possible onto each page.

There are columns and columns of different advertisements. Help Wanted has things like *Wanted: A chambermaid. Must have first-class references. Apply at 125 Atlantic Avenue.*

"Look!" Gus says, pointing. "There's a Lost and Found!"

He reads aloud. "'Ten-dollar reward. Went astray Friday, February 25: large yellow Newfoundland dog; white breast, leather collar, answers to Lion. Return to 272 Court Street, between Congress and Warren, in the Oyster Saloon.'"

Nat grins. "That's so cool! I wonder if Lion was ever found?"

I scan the page. There's a small yellow box highlighting an ad:

Boarding

```
TO LET WITH BED AND MEALS
A very pleasant quite large room. Home has all
modern amenities. Apply at 42 Willow Street.
```

"Well," I say, "it looks like my folks weren't the first ones to rent out that room."

CHAPTER 44

A TERRIBLE TRAGEDY OCCURS

We've gone through about half of the listings. Most are ads through the years for renting out the room. Then my heart skips a beat as the page from 1897 loads and I see the yellow box highlighting the simple headline DIED.

"Wow, they didn't fool around in those days," mutters Gus.

I hold my breath and look. *Spinoza, April 10. After a long and painful illness, John C. Spinoza, aged 45 years and 3 months.*

"Probably not her," Nat declares. I give her a look. "I'm joking."

I turn back to the entries. More rooms to let.

Then I get to April 2, 1909. This time it's page one. The front page.

We scan the headlines: ROOSEVELT LANDS AGAIN, 3 HOURS

AT GIBRALTAR, and HUNTING A FIREBUG——WHITESTONE HAS ONE, AND HE IS BEING EAGERLY SOUGHT.

Nat points at another one. BAKER FINED $100——ADMITTED USING LIQUID EGGS——MILK DEALERS ALSO FINED.

And then I see it. This time the yellow box is part of an article toward the bottom of the page. But the headline in bold letters stops me cold.

Terrible Tragedy as Young Mother Dies in Building Fire

Sari Rosenbaum, 17 years old, was found dead this morning in her apartment at 42 Willow Street, where she was a boarder with her sister.

Mrs. Ryder, who runs the furnished boardinghouse, smelled smoke and called the fire department, who arrived and promptly set to putting out the fire, the cause of which was a faulty gas stove. They came upon a dreadful sight: the bodies of a young woman and a baby boy nearby in his cradle. Mrs. Ryder told the firemen that upon hearing the sirens of the fire engines, Miss Rosenbaum, who had been conversing outside with a young man, rushed into the building to save her baby, only to be overcome by smoke, and she

```
perished alongside her child. Her sister,
Rachel Rosenbaum, 23 years old, had been at
her job as a seamstress. Informed of what
had happened when she returned, she fainted
and had to be revived. Police are still
investigating this incident.
```

All of a sudden I realize I've been holding my breath the entire time I've been reading. Maybe that's why I feel light-headed. I grab the table to steady myself. I look at Gus and Nat, and they both look pretty shaken up too.

"You . . . don't think . . . ?" Gus finally says.

Nat nods. She isn't looking at me; her eyes are glued to the screen. Then I see that she's blinking, and tears are running down her face. It's the first time I've ever seen Nat cry.

"Hey! Are you *crying*?" Gus says, with that incredible talent for saying exactly the wrong thing on any occasion.

Nat wipes her eyes with her sleeve. "So what? It's heartbreaking. Danny was crying too."

I start to protest and then discover that my face is wet. I mean, it really is sad.

"You're an idiot," Nat grumbles to Gus, who looks embarrassed.

"Sari Rosenbaum," I say. "And her sister, Rachel."

Nat keeps looking at the screen. "We need to help her find rest."

"And how do you suggest we do that?" Gus asks.

"She keeps asking where her little boy is," I reply. "We need to find out how to get her to accept that he's not in the apartment anymore."

Nat turns away from the monitor and gathers her things. "We need to talk to her."

"But she'll only talk to Rachel!" I protest.

There is a small "I know the answer" look on Nat's face that I've seen so often in class. "But we've learned her name. Now we can control her."

"That's just something my bubbe said!" I say. "What if she keeps asking for Rachel?"

"Then I'll be Rachel," Nat answers simply.

There is an "I am totally confused" look on Gus's face that I also know from class. "Wait. What?"

Nat looks at me so hard I almost have to turn away. She's got a plan, and I can see there'll be no arguing with her. "She enters the body of people staying in Jake's old room. Danny, you'll stay in the room, and when she comes looking for her son. I'll be there and pretend to be Rachel. Then maybe I can convince her that he's at peace and she'll leave."

"Number one, that's a big maybe," I say. "And number two, you mean you're going to sleep over at my apartment?"

Nat turns red. "Oh, yeah. I guess so. I mean not exactly. We wouldn't be sleeping."

Gus smirks. "Oooh! A *sleepover*? With you two?"

"Shut *up*!" Nat and I say in unison. We look at each other.

"I don't know what is more unlikely," Gus finally says. "You finding a ghost who's going to inhabit Danny and talk to Nat pretending to be her sister, or your parents actually letting you have a sleepover now that we're thirteen."

I have to admit, he has a point.

CHAPTER 45

TWO MOMS WITH A SINGLE THOUGHT

I wait until dinner to bring it up. The look on my mom's face when I ask if Nat can sleep over would be funny except for the fact that it totally isn't.

"Absolutely not." I mean, not even a *second* of hesitation.

"So . . . what? You don't trust me?" I ask.

My dad plays with the food on his plate, not meeting my eye. "It's not that, exactly. . . ."

"Oh, so you don't trust Nat? Really?"

My mom's lips are set in a tight line. "This is completely out of the question. You are thirteen years old. She is not sleeping over."

"But *why*?" I say.

My mom gives me a "you've got to be kidding" look. "Danny, you know darn well why."

"No I don't. Nat and I used to have sleepovers all the time."

"When you were *nine*," my mom reminds me.

"So what's so different now?" I ask.

My dad covers his smile with a napkin. "Um, a little thing called puberty? Maybe you've heard of it, Danny?"

"Oh, for crying out loud!" I squeal. "You two are disgusting!"

My mom lowers the fork she's been jabbing the air with and tries a different tack. "Danny, this isn't about trust. I just don't understand why all of a sudden you two need to have a sleepover."

"It has to do with . . . everything that's been going on," I say. "Nat needs to stay overnight to help me contact the dybbuk."

Dad shoots Mom an accusing look. "Your mother. I could kill her. She's the one who put this idea in your head, Danny, isn't she?"

"Don't blame Bubbe Ruth. Nat, Gus, and I just learned some things about the apartment that might explain what's been going on."

"From whom?" my mom asks suspiciously.

"We went to the Brooklyn Historical Society library, as a matter of fact," I say, trying not to sound as pleased with myself as I am.

My parents exchange glances.

My mom's eyes widen. "You went there on your own?"

"Yes, to do research on the house," I answer.

My dad looks impressed. "Wow. That's a first. Sounds more like something your—"

Mom cuts him off with a look.

"That's okay, Mom, I know Dad was going to say it was something Jake would do. We went because Nat wanted to go. See? She's a really good influence on me."

"Great," my mom says. "You two can go to all the libraries you want together. Just no sleepovers."

Before I can think, the words come out of my mouth. "Mom, you're being ridiculous. Besides, we're not even going to sleep."

Whoops. Really shouldn't have put it that way.

"That's *exactly* what I'm talking about," my mother says triumphantly.

I am trying to ignore the fact that my face is obviously bright red. "I didn't mean that."

"You didn't mean what, exactly?" my dad asks.

"Whatever you're thinking!"

I hate this whole conversation.

Mom's phone rings and she checks to see who's calling, saving me from further humiliation.

Or so I thought.

She looks up after checking the screen. "Ha! That's Marie Haddad. Let's hear what *she* has to say."

Marie is Nat's mother. There is a small part of me willing to hope that she's going to tell my mother she's acting like a jerk and she should trust their children, who have never given them a moment to doubt their moral fiber.

Yeah, fat chance.

My mom is nodding as she looks at my dad. "Yes, Marie. I *know.* I said *exactly* the same thing. I mean, the idea. What? Yes, there have been some events at the house that have been hard to explain, but certainly nothing that would . . . *Right.* No, I don't think that's it. But I'm so glad you called. Of course I'll say hello next time I'm in the store. Goodbye, sweetheart."

Mom clicks off her phone. "Well, Marie is even more dead set against this than we are. She thinks Nat made up the stories about the ghost."

I let out a noise of frustration. I bet there's a word for that noise. I mean, it's not a sigh or a groan. Whatever it is, it drives parents crazy.

"Danny, I *told* her Nat didn't make it up. Just be glad I didn't tell her the truth."

Now I'm getting mad. "What truth? Are you saying I'm lying too?"

Dad steps in. "She's not saying that, Danny. It's just—"

Mom does not appreciate when Dad explains what she's

saying. "I can tell him, dear. Danny, did you hear what your father just did? We call that mansplaining. Don't do that."

"I was *not!*" Dad protests.

"I learned all about that from Nat, Mom. Her sister goes to Barnard, remember?"

Mom softens. "I'm sorry. I know you want to believe there's some sort of evil spirit in this house, but maybe the only evil spirit is that you didn't get the room you wanted. And having Nat over is not going to change that."

I look at Mom, not saying anything. Then I get up, carefully take the plates, and place them in the sink. "May I please be excused?" I ask.

"Sure, sweetheart," my mom says. "And I'm sorry. But really, you've got to trust us that this is not a good idea."

<<*<*<3+

Nothing happened last night. I'm actually a little disappointed. It's like somehow Sari found out that I know all about her and is afraid to show her face. I leave for school before my parents get up, just so I don't have to talk to them. I cannot believe how unreasonable they're being.

At school, Nat looks glum.

It turns out her mother gave her a lecture about "those sorts of boys," and Nat asked her what sorts of boys she meant, and her mom said don't be smart and Nat said you are always telling me how smart I am, and her mom said that's not what I mean, you know what I mean, and Nat said if I knew what you meant I wouldn't ask and that's when her mom called my mom.

It seems we need a plan B.

"Why don't I sleep over?" Gus says, during lunch period.

Nat dips her pita in baba ghanoush. If you've never had it, it's like hummus, but made with eggplant, and it has a smoky flavor. You know what? Even if you *have* had it, you haven't had it like they make it at Haddad's. Trust me.

Anyhow, Nat takes a bite and turns wearily to Gus. "We've been over this. She's not going to believe that you're her sister."

"Why not?" Gus asks, grabbing a piece of pita and dipping it in the baba ghanoush before Nat can slap his hand away.

"Whatever happened to asking?" Nat says. "Gus, you just . . . well, I just think I would be better talking to her, that's all. You know, woman to woman."

Gus does not look impressed. "*You're* a woman? You're a kid."

Nat reddens. "You know what I mean."

We decide to talk more after school, and plan on walking down to Brooklyn Bridge Park again.

Our plans change when we get outside and see my mom and Nat's mom standing there.

"Uh-oh," I say.

Marie Haddad comes up to Nat. She doesn't look mad. Well, maybe a little. "Hi, kids. There's nothing wrong, it's just that we have someplace to go."

In response to our confused looks, my mom adds: "We need to go see your grandfather, Nat. We have been summoned."

The two moms don't seem to know any more than we do what this is about.

CHAPTER 46

THE DYNAMIC DUO SAVES THE DAY

We walk over to Haddad's, Nat's mom complaining the whole way that it's her one day off and her father knows she has things to do, and what's so important that it can't wait until tomorrow. And of course my mom piles on, talking about all the client meetings she had to rearrange. So they're both in a joyous mood.

Nat and I just keep looking at each other like "Isn't this *weird*?"

When we enter the store, Sammy is holding court with a young family. They've just moved to the neighborhood, and he's giving them his list of the best places to eat and shop. Even day care options. But this isn't Sammy being Sammy. It's Sammy being a Brooklynite. Everyone in Brooklyn has an opinion. Like right now, Sammy has just said that the best pizza in the neighborhood is Table 87 and two people in the check-out line butt in to say he is full of it. One saying that the best pizza is My Little Pizzeria and the other says that if you *really* want to get good pizza you have to go to Carroll Gardens.

The couple listens politely. The guy is dark skinned and has his hair in dreads, and the woman has her blond hair in a braid. They've got two kids.

Sammy sees us and allows the two couples in the checkout line to move on from arguing about pizza to arguing about drugstores.

Marie Haddad gives her dad a peck on the cheek, and says, "This better be good, Dad."

Sammy enfolds Nat in one of his bear hugs and claps me on the shoulder. "You don't think I'd drag you down here on your day off for nothing, my precious daughter?"

He kisses my mom on the cheek. "And Maureen! So good to see you, my dear!"

He ushers us to his "office" toward the back and opens the door.

There, behind the desk, is Bubbe Ruth. She has a tray of some of Sammy's finest delicacies in front of her, and it looks like she has polished off about half of them.

Her face lights up when she sees us. "Children! Come! Eat! I can't finish all this."

Nat and I don't wait for our mothers to say anything. We each grab a piece of baklava, and I pop mine in my mouth.

The layers of pastry dough drenched in honey and walnuts fill my mouth with happiness. I know I'm talking like Gus here, but some foods are that good.

"Mom! What are you doing here?" my mother says.

Bubbe Ruth picks up a pistachio cookie. "Noshing, darling. What does it look like?"

"Noshing" is Yiddish for "snacking." You have to hand it to us. We come up with some great words.

Sammy has closed the door and looks on, beaming. Nothing makes him happier than seeing people enjoy the food from his store. I'm just glad Gus isn't here, because the entire tray would be empty in about five seconds.

My mom isn't smiling. "You know what I mean, Mother."

"Sammy sent a car for me, which was wonderful. So much nicer than the bus. I guess that's what people do these days. You can call for a car on your phone and it just shows up! And you don't even pay!" Bubbe Ruth says this like it's a miracle. She notices Nat. "Look at you, Mamele! Such a big girl you've become! And such a beauty! Right, Danny?"

I am amused to see that Nat is blushing. Then I realize I am too.

Now it's Marie's turn. "Very nice, Dad. You want to explain?"

Sammy sits down in his armchair and looks at all of us. "What's to explain? I wanted to see my old friends and my beautiful daughter and granddaughter."

Marie turns to Nat. She does not look happy. "Nat, did you call your *jidoo*?"

Nat calmly cleans the honey from the baklava off her fingers with a paper napkin, which I realize is what I should have done instead of licking them and wiping them on my pants. "No, Mom, of course I didn't."

"You called me, remember?" Sammy tells Marie. "All about this situation where Nat was wanting to stay over at Danny's apartment, and what a ridiculous idea this was."

"Right . . . ," Marie says, her eyes narrowing. She can see where this is going.

"Now, just listen, darling," Sammy admonishes her. "I talked to Nat about it, and—"

Marie whirls on Nat. "I thought you said you didn't call your *jidoo*."

"I didn't," Nat insists. "He called *me*."

"Marie, you never let me finish," says Sammy. "She explained to me the extraordinary circumstances, and I called Ruth to discuss them."

My mom looks at Sammy like he's just grown another head. "You called my mom?"

"It's nice that someone calls. Between you and your brother, I can go weeks without hearing from anybody," Bubbe Ruth says, picking up another pastry.

If my mom's lips were pressed together any harder, they'd be welded shut. This happens whenever this subject comes up. Which it does, frequently. "Mom, I call you every week. And we visit every other Friday."

Bubbe Ruth shrugs. "If you say so."

My mom is about to respond, but Sammy waves her off. "Maureen, darling, this isn't about that. It's about the children. Whether you wish to believe it or not, they clearly feel there is something or someone visiting your apartment at night."

"Yes, but—" Marie tries.

Sammy raises his voice a little. "As I was saying, it's about the children. And trust. Now, we'd like to ask you: Have these two *ever* done anything that would make you not trust them?"

"Exactly," says Nat, crossing her arms. "I always come home when I say I will, do my homework, help out with chores. . . ."

She looks at me. I realize I'm supposed to add my own wonderful qualities.

"Um . . . I've never asked you guys for anything, and I wasn't the one who made a promise and then broke it. That was you. I've never lied to you about *anything.*"

Silence. I am praying my mom doesn't bring up the whole "I'm saying I'm doing my homework when I'm really online playing a game" thing.

But this is about other stuff. Like boy/girl stuff.

Marie and my mom look at each other, then at us, and then back at each other.

Bubbe Ruth is losing patience. "Enough looking, already. These are good children. And they're *children*."

Marie chews her lip. "Well . . . they *are* going to be in separate rooms, right?"

"Absolutely!" Nat and I say at the same time. A little too fast.

"And you're going to be right there," Marie continues, looking at my mom.

Bubbe Ruth has had enough. "Maureen, is this how I raised you? With so little faith?"

My mom bursts out laughing. "Excuse me? When I was Danny's age, if I had so much as *looked* at a boy you would have locked me in my room. You didn't let me date until I was sixteen."

"Who said anything about a date?" Nat says. "This is definitely *not* a date."

"Absolutely," I add.

Sammy kneels down and puts one hand on my shoulder and one on Nat's. Before I know what's happening, he's kissed both of us on the cheek. "I give this my blessing."

There's no way Bubbe Ruth is going to not get in on this. "Come here, children."

She's waving her arms like she's guiding in a plane at JFK.

Nat and I approach her warily. There's no escape. She hugs us close and smooches us. "Respect your parents," she says to my mother and Marie.

My mom looks at Marie and shakes her head. "Well, I guess if it's all right with you, it's all right with me."

Sammy breaks into one of his smiles that can light up the entire store. "There! That wasn't so hard, was it?"

Nat helps him up and gives him a big hug. I hug my mom.

Sammy says, "Now, don't do anything foolish. But I want you to tell me all about it."

Marie looks at Nat. "I don't think your father's going to like this, but that's my problem, I guess."

"Mamele, please. I think you can handle him," Bubbe Ruth says, licking honey off her fingers.

I love her.

CHAPTER 47

WHO'S THAT KNOCKING ON MY WINDOW?

Before we leave Haddad's, Nat has Bubbe Ruth sing "Raisins and Almonds" into her phone. She says she wants to try to learn it before tonight.

Mom and I go home (of course with all sorts of goodies that Sammy insisted we take with us to try and see if we like), and I'm surprised that Dad doesn't seem all that upset about Nat staying over.

"Look, it's different when you're the dad of a girl," he explains.

"Why?" I ask.

He turns red. "Don't they teach you anything in health class?"

"You know girls and boys can just be friends, right?" I ask. "Bubbe Ruth and Sammy seem to have figured that out."

"Believe me, if your mother had asked Bubbe Ruth if she could sleep over at my house when we were thirteen, her head would have exploded," my dad says.

Dad can be unbelievably annoying. "You didn't know each other when you were thirteen."

It's six o'clock, and the buzzer sounds. Nat is here with her dad, George. He's tall and skinny, with a long face and his daughter's dark, knowing eyes. He looks around the apartment after greeting my parents.

"Nice. You painted or something?" he asks.

My mom grabs his arm. "That's right! You haven't seen what we've done to Jake's room!" She drags him back there, proud to show off her work.

Nat laughs. "I don't think my dad has been here since your ninth birthday."

"Why did he bring you instead of your mom?" I ask.

Nat rolls her eyes. "Why do you *think*?" she says.

I hear Nat's dad and Mom coming back down the hallway.

"So . . . Danny is sleeping back there . . . and Nat is sleeping here . . . ," he's saying as he peers into my room.

We don't explain to him that I'm sleeping back there because too many weird things have happened back there, so it's safer for Nat to sleep in my room.

"Wait. He wanted to make sure we weren't sleeping in the same room?" I say softly to Nat.

She sighs. "Mom and I told him like a hundred times."

George looks a little less suspicious. I want to tell him that whatever he's thinking, it's the last thing either of us want to do tonight. But I know it's better to keep my mouth shut.

He sees that my parents' room is across the hall from where Nat is sleeping, and he relaxes a bit. He accepts a glass of wine from my parents, and they sit in the living room and chat. I take Nat to my room, where she puts down her backpack. It's a little weird thinking of her sleeping here.

George leaves, and then we have the most awkward dinner ever. My mom is acting like the mom from some movie, totally not like she's known Nat since she was a toddler. My dad is just awkward and trying to make small talk about school— "So, Nat, what's your favorite subject?"—which makes it sound like he's interviewing her for a job or something.

But Nat is totally cool with it, and by dessert my mom has started to act normal again, although she has to tell Nat the story of how I got ice cream all over myself when I tried to feed it to a stuffed dog I found on the playground, which would have been totally embarrassing, except Nat saves it by saying, "I know. I was there, remember?"

It's great to have friends who've known you so long that they've seen you do stupid things and still hang out with you.

Both my parents have work to catch up on, so they go to their respective laptops and Nat and I go to my room. My parents insist I keep the door open, which is completely dumb. All we're doing is the math assignment. It's actually fun. Nat used to come over after school all the time, but these days she usually goes to Haddad's after school, or goes home with one of her girlfriends, like Lin or Chloe.

Before we know it, my parents are telling us it's time for bed, and I walk to Jake's room.

I expect there to be a feeling in there. Cold air, like before. Or something else.

But nope. It's just a room, with all the new furniture and the prints on the walls. I look at the mirror facing the bed, expecting to see something other than my reflection. Maybe a message written in blood or something.

Nope.

Oh, *great*. So nothing's going to happen? That would be *perfect*. Then not even Nat would believe me.

I put on my pajamas and head to the bathroom. Nat is there, brushing her teeth. This is also weird. Seeing her in her T-shirt and pink pajama bottoms is a first. Her hair is pulled back in a bun, which is not something I expected. She spits in the sink and turns to me.

"What are you looking at?" she asks.

"Nothing," I say, grabbing my toothbrush. I put some toothpaste on it and stick it in my mouth as quickly as possible. I don't know why, but I just don't know what to talk about now.

Nat looks uncomfortable too. "So . . . I'll check in with you later, okay?"

I nod, and she exits the bathroom. I hear her bare feet slapping on the floorboards and then the door to my room closing.

I finish up and head to Jake's room. It's funny how I still call it that.

I settle into the bed. It's nice and big, and having windows is such a new feeling. Obviously I've been in Jake's room thousands of times, but tonight it's different.

There is a soft knock on the door.

"Come in," I say. It's my mom.

"I . . . just wanted to say good night again," she says awkwardly, looking around the room.

I nod. "Okay, Mom. I love you."

She kisses me. "You too, honey. I hope you have a nice restful night."

I try to fall asleep. And I must have drifted off, when I feel someone poking me. It's definitely not a spirit. It's Nat.

"It's me," she hisses, like I wouldn't know.

"I know it's you," I say. "Who else would it be?"

Nat crosses her arms. "I just didn't want you to think I was possessed or anything."

"Fine," I say. "Neither am I, obviously."

Nat sighs. "Obviously." She's clearly disappointed.

We sit there for a few minutes.

"When does it usually happen?" she asks.

"I don't know!" I answer. "I'm always in my room, re-member?"

We sit there for a little while longer. It's starting to feel like this whole idea was ridiculous.

"So . . . ," Nat says, "I guess I should go back to the other room, huh?"

At that moment, there is the unmistakable sound of some-one rapping on the window. From the outside.

CHAPTER 48

A LITTLE GOAT SNOWY AND WHITE

Nat and I slowly turn to look. There, framed in the window, is a face.

Not the pale face of Sari Rosenbaum.

The pink and sweaty face of Gustave Baublitz.

"Gus!" Nat hisses. "What is he doing here?"

I run over to open the window. "You got me. I didn't invite him."

Gus crawls in from the fire escape. "Jeez, it's harder to climb one of those things than it looks."

He looks at our ticked-off expressions. "Nice welcome."

"Why are you here?" Nat asks.

Gus sits on the bed. "Did you think I'd let you guys do this without me? I mean, whatever it is, I just felt that—"

I sit next to him. "It's a very nice thought, Gus, but you should really go home."

Gus crosses his arms. "No way. If that ghost girl shows up, I want to see her."

"Lower your voice!" Nat says fiercely. "If Danny's parents come in here and find me, I'll be sent home for sure!"

Gus sizes up the situation. "Ohhh . . . right. Your parents think you guys are gonna fool around or something, right?"

"Something like that," I say.

Gus grins. "So . . . were you?"

Nat has a look on her face like she's eaten the tuna casserole at school (which I do not recommend, if that isn't obvious). She looks at me and says three words: "Ick. Gross. No."

"Right. Totally gross," I say a little too quickly. Nat looks mad.

"I mean, not that *you're* gross, Nat."

"Just forget it," she mutters.

I do not understand her.

Gus is clearly enjoying every minute of this. "So what's the plan?"

Nat thinks for a second. "We don't really have one. I mean, we have one for if she shows up. We just kind of assumed she would."

Gus thinks for a minute. "When did she come before?"

"Around midnight," I say. "After everyone went to sleep."

Gus lays back on the bed and puts his hands behind his head. "Well, that's that. I guess we have to go to sleep first."

Nat puts her hands on her hips. "Gus, you are *not* staying in this room."

"Oh, who's gonna stop me?" he says, and closes his eyes.

Nat makes a growling noise.

I open the door and peer out. My parents' door is closed. "Listen, Nat, Gus has a point. Why don't you wait outside the door and we'll see what happens if we at least pretend to fall asleep?"

Nat looks over at Gus. "I don't think he's pretending."

Gus is snoring softly and has rolled over on his side.

"I guess all that climbing wore him out," I say.

Nat nods and tiptoes out to wait in the hallway. She closes the door silently behind her, and I settle in next to Gus.

It's kind of like sleeping next to a large golden retriever.

I actually start to doze off after a few minutes, and then I feel something stirring next to me. I assume it's just Gus shifting position, until I hear it.

The walls are whispering, "Yan-kaaa-laaa."

And someone is humming "Raisins and Almonds."

I realize the humming is coming from right next to me. I open my eyes and turn to Gus.

But Gus is no longer Gus. He is glowing faintly and staring at me with yellow eyes.

I sit up. "Sari? Sari Rosenbaum?" Any second now, Nat is going to rush in.

The dybbuk's eyes widen, and she hisses. Then she speaks in the high girlish voice just like before. "Where is my little boy?"

Where is *Nat*? This would be a good time to rush in.

I edge off the bed. Gus follows me, backing me up against the wall. I am trying to yell for Nat, but no sound comes out of my mouth.

I look in the mirror over Gus's shoulder, and I see my own face, eyes wide with fright.

But instead of Gus in the mirror, there is a young woman in a long black dress. I see the braid falling down her back. She turns sideways, and now I see her pale skin is deathly blue white. I recognize her from Katia's photo. The same sad eyes and down-turned mouth.

Sari repeats her question, grabbing me with ice-cold hands. *"Where is my little boy?"*

Where the heck is Nat? Why hasn't she come in?

"I don't know!" I say as loudly as I dare. I hear a bump on the other side of the door, as if someone is getting up.

"Where are you hiding him?" she demands.

As the door opens, I feel her icy hands move to my throat. Nat calls out, "Sari Rosenbaum!"

I am clawing at the hands as they tighten. "I thought if we called her name, it would control her!" I manage to gasp.

Nat rushes over to pull Sari off, but the dybbuk pushes her away.

"Sari! Sari Rosenbaum!" Nat tries again, with no result.

Those cold fingers. Pushing down on my throat. The room is beginning to swim.

Then Nat sings, in English:

> *"To my little one's cradle in the night*
> *Comes a little goat snowy and white.*
> *The goat will trot to the market*
> *While mother her watch does keep,*
> *Bringing back raisins and almonds.*
> *Sleep, my little one, sleep."*

The fingers relax, and the dybbuk steps back, transfixed, as she stares at Nat through Gus's eyes. She turns to Nat and listens. In the mirror I see her sad eyes and pale skin and lace collar.

As Nat finishes singing, she does not take her eyes off the dybbuk, who begins to sing softly.

> *"Unter Yankele's vigele*
> *Shteyt a klor-vays tsigele.*
> *Dos tsigele iz geforn handlen*
> *Dos vet zayn dayn baruf,*
> *Rozhinkes mit mandlen.*
> *Slof-zhe, Yankele, shlof."*

I watch as Sari reaches out and strokes Nat's cheek. Then she speaks.

"Rochele?"

"Yes, I am your sister, Rachel," Nat says.

The dybbuk looks confused. "But why do you sing in English, my sister?"

"We are in America now, Sari. We practice our English."

Sari nods. "Yes, I understand."

Nat turns to me. "When your grandmother sang the song into my phone, she didn't say Yankele, she said yingele. Do you think?"

Of course.

I stand next to Nat and face Sari. "Is Yankele your little boy?"

Her eyes move to mine. It's Gus's face, but the eyes are young, and sad, and old. All at the same time.

Yankele . . . the name whispered by the walls . . .

"Yes, Yankel. That is his name. Where is he? Please tell me."

"But you knew how he—" I begin, and then Nat tugs my sleeve.

"Her son . . . I remember from the paper. His name wasn't Yankel. It was Isaac."

If her son was Isaac, then who is Yankel?

My mind is racing as I try to think of why I know the name Yankel.

Bubbe Ruth would sometimes say it. Was it the name of an uncle?

Yes, that's right.

It was *her* uncle.

Yankel.

The Yiddish version of Jacob.

Who gave his name to his great-niece's son.

Jacob, called Jake.

CHAPTER 49

SARI'S LITTLE BOY

I sit on the bed next to Gus, who turns to face me. I take his hand in mine, pressing my warmth into his cold flesh.

Sari's eyes look back at me, searchingly. She knows I have the answer.

"Your. . . . little boy . . . ," I begin. "He's not your son, is he?"

Sari's yellow eyes glisten. She is lost in memory. "He was . . . my second son."

Nat starts to correct her, but I stop her.

"Yes," I say, "but he came later, right?"

Sari nods. "Much later. I waited so long for him. Years, maybe longer. So many people living in my room . . . sailors, rough men who worked on the docks, even a few women."

"Women?" Nat asks.

"They would come for a few years. The room was never warm, never a place of love. Always a place of loneliness."

I picture this room, as the boarders come and go, working hard during the day, alone at night. The lucky ones would meet someone and move out. The others would just move on to another room, another life. All the Richies and Katias coming to the city to make their mark, or just landing here and never leaving. All being watched by an unhappy spirit unable to move on, needing to love and protect another boy. To get another chance, to make it right this time.

A small smile appears on Sari's lips as she moves forward in her mind. "And then they came. The couple. I hear the sound of a child."

"And that was Jake—er, Yankel?" Nat asks.

Sari shakes her head. "He comes later. This is not my little boy."

That would be my grandparents. I remember seeing pictures. This was their bedroom, when the apartment only had one bathroom. My dad's room was what is now his and my mom's room.

Only after my grandparents moved out and my parents took over the apartment did they renovate and put in the second bathroom, giving this room to Jake.

"The couple leaves, and a crib is brought into your room for the first time," I say gently.

I feel Sari's hand growing warmer in mine. "Yes! Finally! My little Yankel. He is here with me every night."

My brother. All those years. Watched over by his second mother. Who protected him like she couldn't protect her own son.

Tears appear in the corners of Sari's eyes. I want to make clear that this whole thing is amazing, sitting with Gus and talking to someone long dead. After all the terror I've felt these weeks, now all I feel is wonder.

"They called him Jacob, right?" Nat asks.

"Yes, and he is beautiful. And so smart, this one. So much joy for me, watching him grow through the years into a strong handsome boy. I help him sometimes."

"Help him how?" I ask.

Sari is lost in her thoughts. "When he is afraid, I comfort him. When he needs to study, I give him strength and whisper words of support. Like a good mother."

She turns to me. "I was a good mother, wasn't I?"

"He couldn't have asked for a better one," I say.

Nat has to go there. "So . . . there was another little boy who came later, wasn't there?"

Sari's face changes. She wrinkles her nose. "Yes. A noisy and clumsy thing. Not like *my* little boy. This one talked too loud and tried to get Yankel to play with him."

Nat is doing everything she can to not burst out laughing. I poke her.

"Thanks a lot," I mutter.

"Shhh!" Nat giggles.

Darkness clouds Sari's face. "But then Yankel goes. And they take away his bed, his things. They cut out my heart!"

Gus begins to sob. I awkwardly rub his back to comfort Sari.

"I need to know!" Sari says between sobs. "Where is my little boy?"

Nat hugs Gus, which normally would be major news, but I realize she's hugging Sari, which is okay.

"There, there," Nat coos. "Your little boy is just fine. He is so smart he has gone on to a great school to continue his studies."

Sari's eyes light up. "A yeshiva! He has gone to a yeshiva? Perhaps one day he will be a great rabbi?"

I want to tell Sari that it's more likely Jake will be turned into a great rabbit, but I don't want to hurt her feelings. "Something like that," I lie. "He is certainly becoming a great scholar."

"So he is healthy? He is happy?" Sari implores me.

I take out my phone. "Here, I'll show you." I pull up photos Jake has sent us from Cornell. I pass the phone to Gus.

Sari looks down and caresses the phone with her hand.

"Such a handsome boy," she murmurs. Then she kisses the screen.

She turns and shows the photos to Nat. "Is he not handsome?"

Nat turns red. "Yes, he is very handsome."

Sari makes a tsking noise. "Not like the little one. Yech. That one is no prize, am I right?"

Nat is doing everything not to explode at this point. "Oh, yes. Totally."

At this point I really want to think that Gus is just putting on an act, but I know he's not.

Sari wears an expression of concern. "If only I could be sure. If I knew, then I could finally rest."

Nat looks lost. "But . . . we told you . . ."

Sari's eyes go cold. "Like you told me Isaac's death was not my fault, Rachel? You, of all people? You lied to me, Rachel."

Nat bites her lip. "I did it to spare your feelings."

"No, my sister!" Sari snarls. "If I had not stepped out to talk to Nathan from next door, who said such pretty things, my Isaac would have not drowned. It was my selfishness and vanity."

"But you have suffered enough!" Nat insists.

"I am so tired," Sari says. She looks at me, pleading. "I need to see that Yankel is still big and strong and alive. Then perhaps I can rest."

I take my phone back. It's late, but college students stay up late, right?

I pull up the FaceTime app and press the photo of Jake.

There is the sound of the connection, and then the screen shows a darkened room, with a fuzzy voice saying, "Danny? What's up? There a problem?"

"I didn't mean to wake you," I say quickly.

Jake's bleary-eyed face shows up on-screen. "No worries. I was just . . . you know . . ."

"Sleeping?" I ask.

"Mom and Dad aren't there, are they?" Jake demands.

I answer quickly, "No! I'm here with Nat in your old room."

Jake's face changes to a look of astonishment. "What? I mean, that's awesome. Wow, Mom and Dad are getting really broad-minded!"

Nat grabs the phone. "Shut *up*, Jake! It's not like that."

Jake grins. "Hey, whatever you say. My lips are sealed."

I take the phone back. "Listen, Gus is here too, and—"

Now Jake looks really confused. "Wait, what?"

"Look, it's not easy to explain. I just need you to answer a question for me."

Jake stifles a laugh. "Okay. I mean, I thought this stuff was covered in health—"

Nat is about to throw the phone across the room. "Stop being so disgusting, Jake. And listen to Danny."

"Okay, okay."

I try to figure out how to say this without sounding totally insane. "So . . . I know this is going to sound crazy . . . but did you ever have the feeling that there was someone watching over you in your room?"

I don't know what I expected Jake to say, but I wasn't prepared for this.

"Of course," he says. "I've always felt it."

Nat stares at the phone. "Really?"

"I mean, I didn't ever talk about it, because Mom and Dad would have put me in therapy or something, but yeah. Ever since I was little, if I had trouble sleeping, I'd hear this voice singing this lullaby, and it would always calm me."

Jake stops himself. "But wait a minute. How did you find out about it? I never told you."

I sigh. "It's a long story. . . ."

Sari, who has been sitting with her eyes closed, begins to hum.

Jake's face lights up. "That's it! That's the song! Bubbe Ruth used to sing it too! But it wasn't just the song. I don't know how to explain it. It was like a guardian angel was looking over me. I always felt protected in that room. If I was sad, she comforted me; if I was scared, I felt less alone. I kind of thought of her as my second mother."

My voice is barely a whisper. "She's still here, Jake. And she misses you."

Jake pulls the phone close to his face. Something about his expression makes him look like a little boy. "May I speak to her?"

Nat takes the phone. "Listen, Jake, you should know she's speaking through Gus. Which is weird, but that's how it worked out."

Amazingly, Jake just says, "I understand."

Nat hands the phone to Gus, who opens his eyes and gazes down at Jake's face.

"Yankel," Sari murmurs.

"Hello, Mamele," Jake says gently.

"You look tired. Are you working hard?" Sari asks.

"I am doing everything I can to make you proud," Jake answers.

Sari sighs. "So you are good, my darling?"

Jake nods. "Yes, Mamele. I am good. All is well. You have done your job."

Sari smiles. I never thought I'd say this in a thousand years, but right now, Gus looks like Bubbe Ruth. I glance in the mirror and see Sari, tears streaming down her face.

She seems overwhelmed. "That is all I wanted to hear, my dearest one."

"I'll miss you," Jake says, "but I think it's time for you to go."

Sari takes a deep breath. "Yes, I think you are right. I am very tired, and now I can rest."

"Good night, Mamele. Remember what you used to whisper in my ear?"

"Yes, of course, my darling little one." Sari says.

"'The white goat is coming,'" Jake says, "'to bring you raisins and almonds. . . .'"

As he says this, he waves. I press the disconnect button and the phone goes silent.

Gus slowly turns and lies back on the bed.

"I am so sleepy . . . so sleepy . . . ," says Sari as the bed begins to tremble beneath us.

Nat and I jump up and move away from the bed, which is now vibrating.

Sari is sinking into the bed, deeper and deeper.

And then the bed begins to rise . . . a foot or more off the ground.

"If it starts to spin and he pukes, I am *not* cleaning it up," I announce to Nat.

She doesn't answer, transfixed by the scene in front of us.

There is a shaft of light coming through the window. It grows and gets brighter, enveloping Gus's body.

For a second, I could swear I see something jump out of Gus's body and become one with the light, joining whoever or whatever is up there.

Just as the light disappears, the bed slams back to the floor and comes apart. Pieces of it scatter everywhere.

As I hear my parents coming down the hallway, Gus looks up at us. Then he looks down at the mess around him.

"Jeez, I knew Ikea furniture was cheap, but this is ridiculous!"

CHAPTER 50

JUSTICE IS MINE

Try explaining *that* one to your parents.

I hope you have better luck than we did.

I was grounded for a week, and Nat had to promise to work in the store every day after school for a month.

Gus was just smacked in the head by the old man after Emil shrugged and said, "What can you do? He's a crazy kid."

I don't want to leave the impression the old man hit him that hard. It was like what you do to a dog when it makes a mess on the carpet.

But there was a lot of good that came out of it. First off, my dad wrote down everything that happened and showed it to Jack Tempkin, who was convinced it was a perfect movie idea. Jack took it to a friend he knows who produces programs for Netflix, and they *loved* it. So my dad is actually going to make a film about it! And if they like it, they want him to finish his other one!

To no one's surprise, all the weirdness stopped. My mom wouldn't believe that our sleepover had anything to do with it, and made me and Nat promise we wouldn't do that again. We both immediately agreed.

I actually said, "Yeah, like I'm ever going to spend the night with her again."

Nat then called me a name I'd rather not write here. She looked really mad. Which makes no sense because I just wanted to make it clear to my mom, but she seemed to take it really personally.

For the record, I am not completely clueless or stupid. I just can't imagine that someone that smart and pretty would like me. Something else *must* be going on. Maybe when I'm Jake's age it will start to make sense.

But here's the thing: the absolute *best* part was when Mom and Dad were asked to come down to Haddad's on Sunday.

Now this is already strange because Haddad's is closed on Sunday, so I know something is going on. I ask Nat, but she just smiles and says, "You'll see."

When we get there, we see a whole crowd of people in front of the store. Most of them are other store owners, including Emil, who make up the Brooklyn Heights and Cobble Hill Merchants Association. Bubbe Ruth is there too. I go over to give her a kiss.

"Mom! What are you doing here?" my mother asks.

Bubbe Ruth shrugs (what else?). "You couldn't come visit me this Sunday, I thought I'd come to you."

Sammy joins us. I've never seen him in a suit and tie before. I guess he came from church. He waves us over and greets my mom and dad with hugs. There are three chairs behind him, and he indicates that we're supposed to sit.

He clears his throat. He's such a big loud guy that just clearing his throat quiets everybody down.

Sammy glances at his notes. "Good afternoon, everyone, and thanks for coming for this first presentation of the Brooklyn Heights and Cobble Hills Merchants Association Grant for Further Education."

My dad and mom look at each other.

Sammy peers down at them and gives them one of his smiles. Right then and there, I realize it makes sense that he can make the ultimate malted milk ball, because he also makes the ultimate smile.

"In consultation with the other members of our committee, we have decided to put aside a certain sum of money every year from here forward, in order to help deserving families with the burden of paying for college education for promising students from the neighborhood."

I cannot believe where this is going.

"For our first student, we have decided on Jacob Kantrowitz, who is already continuing his studies at Cornell University," Sammy continues.

"Such a genius! *Kein ayin hara* poo poo poo," says Bubbe Ruth, spitting through her fingers. When we told her about Sari, she didn't laugh or shake her head. She simply nodded and said, "I knew that boy had someone looking over him."

Sammy fishes something out of his pocket and unfolds it. "I am pleased to present this check for fifteen thousand dollars to Jacob's parents, Martin and Maureen, to help defray the costs of his education, to be paid yearly until his graduation!"

Sammy hands the check to my stunned father, and everybody claps and hoots, and there's so much noise I can barely hear it when Sammy looks directly at me and says, "Listen, don't you think the kid finally deserves a real room?"

At that point they open the door to the store. They've set up lots of tables with foods from all the merchants on Atlantic Avenue and Court Street laid out. People from Brooklyn sure love to eat.

I go up to Nat, who is with Gus, who has piled a plate with about five pounds of food.

"Did you know about this?" I ask her.

"Maybe," she says, giving me a small smile. I think she's still mad at what I said.

"You know what I said about never spending the night with you again?" I ask.

Nat stands there, not giving an inch. "What about it?"

"I couldn't have done it without you. I'm really glad you slept over."

Nat's face turns redder than the tomatoes on Gus's plate. "You are an idiot. I don't even know what to say to that."

She stomps off and I turn to Gus.

"Don't look at me," he says. "I thought it was a nice thing to say."

Anyhow, that's how I got Jake's room.

I mean, my room.

I guess I'll have to get used to saying that.

Now that my parents have the money to help Jake, we're stopping with the AirHotel. Like I said, Dad got something called an option from Netflix on his screenplay about the Brooklyn dybbuk. Although I'm not totally sure what that means, it *does* mean that he's gotten money for something he's written, and it might become a movie, so that's pretty great too.

And even Mom agrees that having all those strangers in her house was cool but a little hard with a full-time job and everything.

We do have one more person who is staying in the room before I can get it.

Mr. Rosen is an old man from Philadelphia, whose wife

is having surgery at Maimonides Medical Center. Once she's discharged, they'll stay with their daughter. But the daughter has to be out of town for a meeting the night of the surgery, so he's staying with us. He made the reservation a month ago, and we didn't have the heart to cancel on him.

When Mr. Rosen arrives, he turns out to be very nice and a little shy. I think he's worried about his wife. Mom helps him bring his suitcase (I don't think he travels very often—the suitcase is blue plastic—I've only seen ones like it in movies from the 1970s) to his room, asking all about his wife's procedure. My mom is the best at talking to people. That's what makes her such a good social worker. Maybe I should ask her about talking to Nat.

Nah, that's probably a bad idea.

But Mr. Rosen loves talking with her, and all through dinner (he is delighted to be invited to join us) he talks about his wife and which television shows she loves. He is fascinated by Dad's work, of course. But then he turns to me and says, "So, young man, what are *you* interested in?"

For what feels like the first time ever (my parents will insist I'm exaggerating, but I'm pretty sure I'm not), I get to talk about things I like. So it's a great evening.

I walk by Jake's—*my* room and listen hard, but there are no whispers.

After taking my shower, I check the mirror. No messages.

I climb into bed, realizing that this could be one of the last times I'll be in this tiny little closet.

I'll kind of miss it.

Okay, not really. I feel my eyes drooping, and I know I'll be getting a nice, restful night's sleep.

Some time later, I am awakened by a knock on my door.

It can't be happening again.

The door opens, and there stands Mr. Rosen. He opens his mouth to speak.

"Listen, young man, the toilet doesn't seem to flush right. You think you can look at it?"

I sigh and follow him.

This I can handle.

ACKNOWLEDGMENTS

I am Brooklyn born and raised. If you walk the brownstone-lined streets of Brooklyn Heights, the history of all who lived here calls out to you. There was no doubt in my mind that if I was going to write a ghost story, it would be set in this place. Brooklyn has always been a borough with one foot in the past and one in the future, and seeing the great diversity of the people who live, work, and rub up against one another on a daily basis has been an inspiration to me since I was a kid. To the people of Brooklyn, a big thank-you.

The story of the Lebanese Christians who have lived in downtown Brooklyn for more than a century isn't as well-known as Italian or Jewish Brooklyn immigrants, but it is no less compelling. I would never presume to tell their story (as a firm believer that authentic voices must come from the community itself) but am so grateful that the Sahadi family allowed me a small window into their lives, especially

Ron Sahadi and Christine Sahadi Whelan, who now run their father Charlie Sahadi's business. Christine was especially valuable in giving me details about everything from her parents' struggles during the early days of the store to the correct pronunciation of *Gedu,* their family word for *Grandfather.*

A big (but quiet) thank-you to Cecily Dyer, reference librarian at the Brooklyn Historical Society, for her help and guidance in discovering the best way for Danny, Nat, and Gus to research the history of apartment 2R.

As always, I need to thank my agent, Holly Root, who is never more than an email or phone call away, keeping the ghosts of book deals gone bad at bay.

As for my tireless editor, Kate Sullivan, who is no doubt haunted by my insistence on telling more than showing and whose bloodred pencil marks would send chills into even the most intrepid writer, my undying thanks. I am sure she would want me to cut at least one of those ghostly references, but too bad!

And a big nod of thanks to girl wonder, editorial assistant Alexandra Hightower, who deserves an entire bag of ultimate malted milk balls for her good humor and patience in helping to get this manuscript in shape.

Heather Hughes and Colleen Fellingham, demon copyeditors, long may you catch all my errant grammatical missteps. If I've misspelled anything or gotten anything factually wrong in these acknowledgments, you've found those as well, no doubt!

Our designer Michelle Cunningham deserves all praise for bringing brilliant cover artist Marco Guadalupi to the project, as well as all other labors in making the book you are holding now.

Finally, I cannot thank my loving and supportive parents, Robert and Joan Markell, enough for deciding to *not* move to the suburbs or the West Coast but staying put, letting me and my sister, Marni, grow up in what was a very different Brooklyn Heights, giving us a place filled with books, art, and nightly stories and laughter around the dinner table.

I have had the enormous privilege of watching our now-teenage son Jamie grow up in the same neighborhood I did, walking the same streets, buying snacks from some of the same stores, and even attending the same school.

To that street-smart young man and his mother, my beloved wife and partner, Melissa Iwai, always go the biggest thank-yous.

And to all the ghosts of Brooklyn, long may you haunt our stories and imaginations.

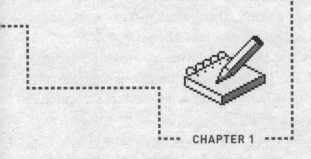

CHAPTER 1

WHO KNEW A MAN WITH TUBES IN HIS NOSE COULD BE FUNNY?

It looks like something from a science-fiction movie, with so many machines and tubes going into and out of bags hung on poles.

For a moment, it doesn't register that all those tubes and hoses are connected to a person.

I have no memory of what he looked like when I was little, and the only photo of Great-Uncle Ted in our house is from ages and ages ago. It shows a burly man with a crew cut, sitting in a living room in the 1960s. He's got a cigarette in one hand and a lighter in the other. I wonder if he hadn't smoked so many cigarettes maybe he wouldn't be here now. He's looking at the camera with a confident grin that says this is not a man to mess with. The only other place I've ever seen Asian men with kick-butt expressions like that is in samurai or martial-arts movies.

Not that I watch them all that much.

I mean, it's bad enough other people make assumptions about us Asian kids. No need for me to help out.

But I gotta say, that photo can't be further from the old man lying in this bed. The grossest thing is the tube going right up into his nose. It looks horrible, and is attached to a machine that does who knows what.

I go and stand awkwardly by the window, unsure of what to do. I wish Mom had come in with me, but she said Great-Uncle Ted wants to see me alone. Dying man's last wish and all, I guess. I clear my throat and sort of whisper, "Um, hi?"

"Arwhk."

The two veiny sacs of his eyelids slowly open, and when he sees me, he gestures, beckoning me over with one hand.

I gingerly approach the chair next to his bed, careful not to disturb any of the wires and tubes snaking around him. It's hard—I have visions of knocking into some hose or other just as I'm supposed to be having a nice visit.

"Gghhh . . ." Great-Uncle Ted catches my eye and reaches out.

Without thinking, I flinch. I have a flashback to a movie I saw where a guy laid out like this had a monster burst out of his chest and jump on someone's face. I'm not saying I expect that to happen here, but hey, it does go through my mind.

Great-Uncle Ted's eyes change. He points impatiently to something on the table.

A pad and paper. There is spidery writing on it.

"You want me to . . . give you the pad?" I ask.

Now there's a flash of fire in Great-Uncle Ted's eyes. I know when someone's ticked off. The message is clearly *Yes, you idiot. Give me the pad.*

I hand the pad to my great-uncle, who winces in pain as he presses a button on the side of his bed that raises him to a seated position.

Slowly, he writes something and then hands me the pad.

Hurts too much to talk. You Amanda's boy, Ted?

I start to write an answer on the pad.

The next thing I know, Great-Uncle Ted yanks the pad out of my hands. The old dude is surprisingly strong!

BEEP BEEP BEEP

Great. Now the heart-rate machine is going a lot faster. That can't be good.

He scribbles something and hands the pad back to me.

I'm not deaf, you little dope. Talk to me.

I laugh in spite of myself. Of course. Duh.

"Yes, uh, sir . . . I'm Ted." I feel a little weird introducing myself, since *he* knows who I am, but since I don't remember him, it feels like the right thing to do. And I'm pretty sure he seems like a "sir."

The old man writes some more. He's writing with more energy now.

You got big. Do you still like playing games?

"What games do you mean, sir?" I ask.

Kissing games.

What th—?

"Uh, no, sir," I begin. "I don't enjoy kissing games. That is, I've never played them. Maybe I would enjoy them if I did. I mean, you never know about something until you try it, right?" I'm babbling now. Trying to look casual, I lean against something, then realize it's a pole holding some fluid going into my great-uncle (or maybe coming out of him—hard to tell). Gross. I attempt to cross my legs, but I dare anyone to try to do it while wearing these ICU snot-green-colored clown pants they made me wear over my jeans to come in here. It's not so simple. So my leg sort of hovers half hoisted.

Meanwhile, Great-Uncle Ted is scribbling away.

I know you like computer games, you little twerp. I just wanted to see your face.

I laugh, and I see a hint of a smile under all the machinery.

You like the ones where you shoot people?

"I'm not allowed to play those," I say, which is the truth.

I didn't ask if you were allowed to. I asked if you liked them.

I smile and nod. This guy is pretty sharp. "Um . . . yeah, I play them sometimes."

Great-Uncle Ted looks at me with an expression I can't make out.

A lot of fun, huh?

"I guess." I shrug.

I hope that's the only way you ever have to shoot and kill a man. The other way is a lot less fun.

"You've killed a man?" I try to ask casually, but it kind of comes out in a squeak. Not my most macho moment, but give me a break, I wasn't ready for this.

Quite a few, yes.

What did Uncle Ted *do* before he retired? I wonder what sort of professions call for killing men. Or more precisely, "quite a few" men. Was he a soldier? A *hit man*?

Let's talk about something else. Why do you like these games so much?

I'm happy to move on. "I don't think the shooting games are all that—and that's the truth. It's more something to do with my friends when we hang out. What I really like is what are called escape-the-room games."

Tell me about them.

Sure, why not? "They're kind of puzzles, where you're stuck in a room and have to figure a way out."
Great-Uncle Ted's eyes survey the space around him.

There's only one way to escape this room.

"Well, I don't agree," I say eagerly, standing up to look around. "There are all sorts of exits, if you look carefully. Not just the door. There's that window. You could tie your sheets together and climb down there, or maybe there's an air-conditioning duct—"

TAP TAP TAP.

My brilliant analysis is interrupted by the sound of my great-uncle's pencil tapping loudly on the pad to get my attention.

I was actually referring to dying, Ted. Try to keep up.

I sit down, deflated. "I guess I didn't think of that," I say honestly, "because you seem so alive."

Great-Uncle Ted does his best to roll his eyes.

Don't bother sucking up to a dying man, Ted. You any good at these room games?

"Never seen a game I couldn't solve or beat. I'm always the top scorer—that means I've solved them quicker than anyone else. I guess that makes me the best," I say, before realizing how obnoxious it sounds. "That sounds like bragging. Sorry."

You ever heard of Dizzy Dean?

Okay, that's a little random. But old people do that some-times. The name does sound kind of familiar, but I can't place it. I shake my head.

One of the best pitchers in the history of baseball.
When you go home, look up what he said about bragging.

Great-Uncle Ted settles back onto his pillow. He's clearly tired.

I stare out the window, watching the headlights of the traffic below making patterns on the ceiling. "Yeah. That's about the one thing I am good at," I say softly, almost to myself. I hear scratching, and he's up and writing more.

Don't ever sell yourself short, Ted. Your mother says you're
very smart.

I nod my head and laugh. "Yeah, I know, I just don't 'apply myself.' She's always saying that. Lila's the smart one."

Lila is my big sister, the bane of my existence. Lila the straight-A student, Lila the president of the student body. Lila, who got the highest Board scores in La Purisma High's history. Lila, who gave the most beautifully written senior address at her graduation, currently crushing it in her freshman year at Harvard. I mean, seriously. Why even try to compete with that?

Your mother told me you're smarter than your sister. You just
don't know it.

Oh, snap! I hope there's a burn unit at Harvard, because Lila just got *smoked.* Big-time!

I'm starting to like Great-Uncle Ted. But I feel bad. We've been talking about me the whole time I've been here. Well, except for the part about him killing a lot of people. I'm pretty sure I don't want to hear more about that.

"So I guess you knew my mom when she was a little kid," I begin. "What was she like?"

Amanda was a pain in the a

He stops and his eye drifts up to my face and back down to his pad.

Amanda was a pain in the ~~a~~ behind, if you'll excuse my French.

I can't believe I thought this was going to be boring. This is *great*! "Seriously? How so?" It takes all the self-control I can muster to get this out without cracking up.

He writes for a long time, then hands the pad to me.

When she was nine, she had this thing where no matter what you would ask her she'd say, "That's for me to know and you to find out."
Like you'd ask her, "What flavor ice cream do you want?"
"That's for me to know and you to find out."
"What movie do you want to see?"
"That's for me to know and you to find out!"
"Do I have lung cancer?"
"That's for me to know and you to find out!"

I choke at that last one.
Great-Uncle Ted waves his hand wearily.

*I made that last one up. But she did say it all the time. She
thought it was cute. It stopped being cute after the first day.
Then it was annoying as heck.*

Great-Uncle Ted pauses.

But she was always smart. And I'm very proud of her.

Great-Uncle Ted was the one who paid for Mom to come to
California from Hawaii and go to nursing school. She's been
working here at La Purisma General Hospital for as long as I
can remember.

Great-Uncle Ted looks up from the paper, and his wise, half-
lidded eyes meet mine. He scrawls on the page and holds up
the pad.

*Please tell me about the games you play. How you solve
these puzzles.*

Wait. Is a real, live adult person actually asking me *details*
about the games I play? This is unheard of.

So I go on and on, explaining how the games work, how at
first nothing seems to make sense. But then, as I put my mind
to it, a little click goes off in my head and the pieces begin to
fit. It's an awesome feeling when it all comes together and you
get it right.

Great-Uncle Ted seems genuinely interested, especially
when I tell him about a particularly tricky puzzle, where if you
look carefully at what appears to be a bunch of random drinking glasses on a tray, you realize they actually resemble the

hands of a clock set to a particular time. Which is one of the main clues to solving that game.

"You know, maybe if they let me, I can come back tomorrow with my laptop and show you some," I'm saying, when I see that his head has fallen back onto the bed and his eyes are closed. "Great-Uncle Ted! Are you all right?" I gasp. "Should I get Mom?"

He wearily reaches for the pad and writes carefully.

I'm just tired. But I'm happy to see you again, Ted.

"I—I'm so glad I could talk to you too, sir," I say, feeling my breathing slow down again.

I feel so much better about everything now. You are ready.

Huh? What does that mean?
"That's good, sir."
The old man looks up at me. The energy is clearly draining out of him.

You must promise me one thing.

"I know, sir. I promise I'll work harder in school, and I'll never tell Mom you thought she was a pain in the behind—"
I think he'll laugh at this, but instead, he gathers his strength and writes furiously across the pad.

No! Listen to me! You must promise me

He's writing slower now, forcing the words out of the pen.

"Yes, sir?"

Great-Uncle Ted falls back and throws the pad at me.

*THE BOX IS ONLY THE BEGINNING. KEEP LOOKING
FOR THE ANSWERS. ALWAYS GO FOR BROKE!
PROMISE ME!*

With great effort, he tugs on my sleeve. I lean toward him. He pulls me down until my ear is close to his face. I can just make out the word he is saying.

"Promise!" the old man croaks. He releases my sleeve. He looks peaceful now, like a weight has been lifted off his shoulders.

As my great-uncle falls asleep, I hear my own voice, sounding far away, whispering, "I promise."